MIASMA

JESS HYSLOP

LUNA NOVELLA #16

Luna
Press
PUBLISHING

Text Copyright © 2023 Jess Hyslop
Cover © 2023 Jay Johnstone

First published by Luna Press Publishing, Edinburgh, 2023

www.lunapresspublishing.com
ISBN-13: 978-1-915556-01-1

To my family.

Contents

Chapter One

The first time I saw an unmasked mage I ran whimpering back into the house.

Balx was standing in the doorway. "Hsst!" he grunted. "Where you off to, boy?" He tried to catch me, but the horror that clutched me was stronger than his great hands. I dodged him and squeezed past, scampering through the front room and into the bedroom. There I halted, back pressed against the door, trembling with relief.

But as my shock abated, shame rose in its place. I was already failing Ma. I'd promised myself that I'd be brave when the mage arrived, for her sake. For the past three days I'd rehearsed the meeting in my mind over and over, picturing myself walking out as our visitor dismounted, extending a steady hand and a solemn, grown-up welcome. I'd even steeled myself for the sight of the reptile, all decked out in its saddle and harness. But I hadn't reckoned on the mage arriving maskless. Confronted with that, my small supply of courage had shrivelled like a mootbloom in summer.

By the time I plucked up the nerve to return, Balx had seen to the mage's mount and shown the guest into the front room. The mage's mud-spattered cape hung upon a peg, looking queer and foreign next to my tattered jacket and Ma's old overcoat. The mage herself stood in the middle of our threadbare rug. She was very tall and very thin, straight as a fencepost except where her left shoulder dipped forward slightly, giving her arm a crooked aspect. Her breeches and jerkin were plain and travel-stained. She was buckling on her mask.

"I must apologise," she was saying. "I didn't know there would be a child here."

"That's Nereus," Balx told her.

"The son?"

Balx grunted assent. The mage glanced at me as I peeped around the doorframe. It was an effort not to shrink away again. The mask she'd donned didn't fool me—I was ten years old, I wasn't stupid. Though the scuffed leather concealed the mage's features, even reaching round across her ears and up over the crown of her head, I knew that beneath that blank visage still lurked the face I'd seen outside. I'd only glimpsed it for an instant before wrenching my eyes away, but that was enough to sear it into my memory: the skin crazed with a dense tracery of black veins, hair sparse and patchy on a discoloured scalp, lips the green-black of stagnant water.

"I'm sorry I startled you," the mage said. Emerging through the mask's mouth-grille, her voice was soft and scratchy, like the scrabbling of the many-legged insects that scuttled across our shutters at night. She wore gloves of the same dark leather as her mask.

I gripped the doorframe, anchoring myself against the urge to flee. *Ma*, I thought. *Remember Ma*. My mother needed this woman, no matter how frightening. She needed the gifts the mage possessed, the talents gained through suffering and disfigurement. And Ma needed them because of me.

I forced myself to meet the mage's gaze. Visible through the eyeholes of the mask, her irises were as unnaturally dark as her lips, her pupils lost in them like pebbles thrown into twin black pools.

I swallowed. "Sorry for being rude, Maestress," I whispered.

The mage inclined her head, a grave acceptance. "Nereus," she said. "You are the one who called for aid?"

I nodded, hesitantly, and sidled around the doorframe to stand within the room.

She nodded back. "Good. Then shall we?"

My eyes widened as she removed her gloves. The mage's hands were covered in the same black veins as her face, as though some unknown breed of spider had spun a dark web beneath her skin. Not only that, but across the back of her right hand was a patch of hardened skin, knobbly and dark. Her nails were black too, thick and horny; they put me in mind of a reptile's claws.

She offered her right hand to me. "My name is Charis Yondarin," she told me solemnly. "I come as summoned, and I will serve."

My stomach flipped. The rote words. I was half triumphant and half terrified that she had addressed them to me instead of Balx. Now it was my duty to answer, to complete the exchange. Yet, although I knew it had to be done, I hesitated. It seemed an ominous step, entering into a contract with a mage.

For Ma. Be brave for Ma.

I saw Balx shift beside the mage, and that decided it. I stepped forward and took the mage's hand, trying not to think too hard about the textures I felt beneath my fingertips. "My name is Nereus Vestryn," I said, stammering a little over the formal tone. "I am the summoner, and I will pay."

A subtle sensation ran through me, a hint of warmth that rippled from my palm up through my arm, then crept across my chest and plunged into my heart.

I jerked my hand away with a gasp. I had done it. The deal was made.

The mage ignored my reaction. "And where is your mother, Nereus?"

"Lya's through here," Balx broke in before I could reply. He grasped the mage's elbow and steered her towards the bedroom.

A jolt of annoyance shot through me despite my fear. Ma was my mother, not Balx's; helping her was my responsibility, even the mage had understood that. Balx had nothing to do with Ma, not really. He wasn't related to her, wasn't married to her. He was just some meddlesome man from the village who'd taken to sniffing around our holding. You couldn't even call him a neighbour—we didn't have any of those out here on the swamp's fringes, our house being the last surviving remnant of the old farm holdings. The only reason Balx knew us at all was because the water-pump had seized up last winter and had been too stiff for Ma to free it herself. We wouldn't even have needed to ask him for help if I'd been bigger.

My irritation was short-lived. As I followed the adults into the next room, anxiety swallowed everything else.

*

Ma had not moved since we left to greet the mage, but the sight of her was still distressing. Before this, I couldn't remember the last time Ma had slept past daybreak or taken to her bed before sundown. Now here she was, sprawled on the pallet in the broad light of day, her head thrown sideways on the pillow. I had struggled alone to change her into her nightgown (I wouldn't allow Balx to help, though he had offered), though now it was rucked and twisted about her legs. Sweat dappled her limbs and her flushed face, and despite the open shutters the room was sour with it. Her eyes were closed, but not in peace: the lids twitched and fluttered as though she were trapped in a nightghast. Her mouth was slightly open, a thin trail of moisture creeping from the corner of her lips as her breath rasped in and out.

It was that trail of spittle that upset me most. It seemed obscene, transgressive somehow. It made Ma vulnerable in a way I couldn't articulate.

Balx manoeuvred his bulk around the bed, shuffling to the far side to make room for the mage. He took Ma's limp right hand and stroked it with his thumb. The motion was not tender but hard, almost aggressive, as though he were trying to animate Ma's body through sheer force of will.

I headed to the corner nearest the door and stood with my back pressed against the wall. Immediately I felt like a coward. I took a step forward and attempted to take charge.

"She's sick," I began, but then balked. What should I say? What could I say?

She's sick because of me. She's sick because I stole the helm. I stole the helm to play with, though I knew it was wrong, and now Ma has poison inside of her.

The truth wallowed within me. I knew I could not confess. I was scared of getting into trouble, yes, but it was more than that. It was the helm.

The helm was a secret. I wasn't sure why, but it was. I knew because Ma had always kept it hidden and because, before the swamp's toxins overpowered her, she had made me promise that I would do the same.

"No matter what," she had croaked. "No matter what you're asked, you don't tell anyone about that helm. You put it back where you found it, and you keep it hidden, and you don't tell *anyone*. You understand? You understand, Nereus?"

I hadn't understood, not really. But I had promised.

Now I was stuck, bound by my vow. I could offer no explanation about Ma's condition. I could do nothing but let the mage inspect her and hope beyond all hope that it was not too late.

I sagged back against the wall, wretched in my helplessness. The mage glanced at me, but the look was too fleeting to read an expression in her eyes. Balx ignored me entirely.

"We sent for you as soon as we could," he said. "She's been like this three days, and we don't even have a saluber in the village." There was a note of accusation in his voice, as though the mage was somehow to blame for the distance between here and the citadel whence she'd come.

If the mage noticed his belligerence she did not show it. Pulling up a stool, she sat beside the bed and leaned in to examine Ma. The inspection was practised and methodical. The mage shifted her attention around Ma's body, scrutinising, manipulating limbs, pressing cautiously. When she reached Ma's torso she tilted her head sideways and brought it close to Ma's chest. Fine mesh ovals were set into each side of her mask, and through one of these she listened intently to Ma's jagged breaths.

I hugged myself in my corner, guts churning with worry.

When the mage straightened, Balx could not contain himself. "How bad is she? Can you—"

"Please," she silenced him. "Wait."

Balx obeyed, though his tensed jaw betrayed the effort it took.

I bit my lip as the mage's hands continued to move over Ma. It was hard to believe such ugly things intended anything but harm. But when the mage took Ma's hand in her own, she did so gently. More gently than Balx, that was certain.

The mage tilted Ma's hand slowly to and fro, and then probed, one by one, at her cuticles. "The discolouration is minimal," she observed, "and I can see no hardening. We may be in luck."

I caught my breath, and Balx's eyes lit up. "That's good," he said. "That's good."

The mage laid Ma's hand back down on the bed, then pressed a palm to Ma's forehead. "There has been no bleeding? None from the nose? The eyes?"

"No, no. Thank the Hale, no."

"Then that is more good news." The mage leaned back on her stool, her pose thoughtful. "She went into the swamp," she said. It wasn't a question.

Balx took it as an accusation. "I wasn't here. I've no idea what possessed her."

"So you don't know how long she was out there?"

"No." He shrugged, angry at his own ignorance. "The first I knew of it was when I came round here on Welsday to bring Lya some milk. Good thing I did, too. Found the boy dragging her up the steps. Or trying to, at any rate."

"Nereus?"

I froze as the mage looked round at me. Her stare made me suddenly afraid that she knew everything. Who could tell what mages were capable of?

"Nereus?" she repeated. "Do you know how long your mother was out in the swamp?"

I dropped my gaze to the floorboards, my misery intensifying. The truth was that I didn't know how long Ma had been out there, not exactly, because it was me she'd come looking for in the first place. I did have a rough idea though—perhaps enough of an idea to help the mage with her cure. And yet if I admitted that, I'd only open myself up to further interrogation. I'd already lied to Balx for three days, claiming that I'd had no idea where Ma was before I found her, sickened and inarticulate, crawling back to the house. Balx would be suspicious if I contradicted that story now. Though, if I didn't speak up, the consequences could be even worse.

My eyes sought out Ma, taking in anew her pained grimace, her sweat-soaked hair strung in ribbons across the pillow, that line of drool leaking down her chin.

No. I couldn't stay silent. I had to put this right.

I thought fast, seeking desperately for a compromise. "I don't know exactly," I mumbled. "I just missed her of a sudden, so I went looking, and there she was coming out of the swamp. But it can't have been that long, 'cause I'd seen her a while before. A half-wick, maybe—I mean a chime," I corrected myself, remembering that in the citadel they had clocktowers with pealing bells rather than rough marks notched in candle wax. "Wait, less. A little less than a chime." It was a roundabout way to the truth, as far as I knew it.

The mage nodded slowly. "That makes sense. Yes. That seems about right." Her tone was guileless, but her dark gaze lingered on me a few moments longer before she turned back to Ma.

"Well? Can you help her?" Balx demanded.

The mage stood and pushed away the stool. "Yes," she said. My heart leapt.

"This will require some concentration," the mage continued. "If you would just step away…"

Balx released Ma's hand reluctantly and moved back as best he could in the confined room. I remained in my corner, trying my best not to squirm with excitement and anxiety. Whatever the mage was going to do, whatever she demanded in payment, it was worth it if it made Ma better. I comforted myself with that thought. Soon all would be well again. Soon I could leave my guilt behind.

The mage took both Ma's hands this time. She folded them carefully across Ma's belly and held them there. Ma made a small noise of protest. The mage paused, and after a moment Ma quieted again. Once the mage was sure her patient was calm, she leaned slowly over the pallet.

Discomfort wormed through me as the mage's face drew close to Ma's. Although I knew the mage was helping us, the thought of that terrible face so close to my mother's made me shudder. It didn't help that from where I stood I could not even see the eyeholes of the mage's mask, only a sinister, featureless head bowed over Ma's prone form.

With her face positioned precisely above Ma's, the mage sighed out a long, low breath. Then, abruptly, she inhaled, sucking violently in through her mouth as though no amount of air would be enough to sustain her.

"Hale preserve us," Balx whispered.

I said nothing. My throat was tight with fear. I could only stare at the scene unfolding before me.

A dark smog was seeping from Ma's mouth, drawn by the mage's inhalation. It had the smutty texture of smoke, the bruised colour of storm clouds. It oozed upwards from Ma's lips and vanished into the mage's mouth-grille. At first it was just a trickle, but soon it came thicker, spilling from Ma's body in a gathering stream.

The mage paused, let out a short cough, inhaled again.

An acrid reek filled the room. My nostrils stung and my eyes watered, but I swiped the moisture away and kept watching, fascinated and appalled.

The miasma. So that was what it looked like, once it had taken hold of a victim. That was what we lived in fear of, out here at the swamp's edge.

The dark smoke continued to pour from Ma and into the mage, but after a while the stream began to diminish again. The outflow became more ragged, ebbing in dribs and drabs.

My fists clenched at my sides. It was working. It was horrible to watch, but it was *working*.

Then Ma's eyes opened. The lids snapped back and she stared for a frozen instant at the mage's masked face poised above hers. Then there was a great crack, a blast of evil smog, the sharp smell of lightning—and the mage was flung backwards to crash into the wall.

The pallet groaned as Ma surged upwards, leaping into a crouch like an animal ready to pounce or flee. The tendons in her neck stood out like ropes pulled taut. Her eyes were twin pits of darkness.

I slid to the floor, numb with terror.

The mage staggered to her feet, just in time to throw an arm across Balx's chest as he sprang towards the bed. "No!" she snapped. "Don't touch her." Pushing him back, she advanced warily. A sound started in Ma's throat: a low, continuous snarl, like nothing I had ever heard a person make before.

"Ma?" I whispered.

"Stay there, Nereus." Despite the attack she'd just endured, the mage's voice was steady, as were her hands as she halted at the foot of the bed and raised them slowly before her. She shifted her feet into position too—one slightly forward, one back.

I blinked, incredulous. That was a fighting stance. I'd seen its like a few months before, when a grizzled former footsoldier had passed through the village and the older lads persuaded him to teach them some basic martial forms. Was the mage going to tackle Ma with her bare hands? Pummel her into submission? Get her in a lock and break her arm?

"No," I found myself saying, hoarsely. "You need to get the poison out, not fight her."

"Quiet," the mage said. Her tone brooked no argument.

She flexed her fingers. I glanced at them, then looked back, eyes widening. The mage's black veins were changing, the darkness lightening until her blood glowed with a dim silver light. The change emerged from beneath the mage's sleeves and raced over her hands, radiating across her palms and wrapping around her fingers. I stared, half-awed, half-revolted. It was like she had pulsing silver caterpillars crawling through her.

Ma had seen it too. Her snarl rose in pitch and she leaned back on her haunches. The muscles in her calves tensed visibly. That was all the warning we got before she leapt.

I shrieked. Balx roared. The mage braced—

—and caught her. Silver-veined hands shot out, grabbing Ma's arms as she launched herself forwards. Jolted to a rough halt, Ma yowled in surprise and indignation. She tried to free herself, throwing her weight from side to side, gnashing her teeth, clawing at the mage's arms and torso. But the mage did not relinquish her hold. She clung on grimly, holding her struggling assailant before her. The caterpillar-like tendrils pulsed brightly; they seemed to be lending her strength.

Then the mage gave a small hiss of effort and the silver light began to fade. The change began at the mage's fingertips, then moved down along the luminescent veins. The silver glow tarnished, then dulled to black, leaving the mage's hands once more webbed with darkness.

Even terrified as I was, I realised what was happening. The mage was leaching the toxins out of Ma and taking the evil into herself.

Ma loosed one last furious howl as the remaining poison drained from her. Then, abruptly, she went limp in the mage's grip.

The mage stumbled as the resistance fled from her attacker, but caught herself short of falling. Her arms were trembling now as they supported Ma's weight. Still, the mage did not let my mother drop. One hand came round to support Ma's neck, and she gently lowered her back upon the pallet.

Holding back tears of shock, I inched forward to peer at Ma. For the first time in three days, she looked peaceful. Her eyes were closed once more, and though sweat still soaked her nightgown her breathing was no longer laboured. Her limbs lay soft upon the sheets. All the tension, all the wildness, had left her.

"What happened?" I had never seen Balx so pale. He stood by the wall where the mage had pushed him, eyeing Ma uneasily. "What was that?"

"A final defence," the mage replied quietly. She brushed a strand of hair from Ma's forehead. "One last attempt to retain its host."

"Is she better?" I asked.

The mage stepped away. "Yes. She's better."

"Thank the Hale!" Balx blurted. He staggered to the bedside and fell to his knees, already reaching for Ma.

I yearned to do the same. I wanted to run to Ma and hug her—just hug her and hug her and tell her it was all right now, we'd done it, she was cured. But I couldn't do it, not with Balx crushing Ma's hand in that possessive way of his. His presence repelled me even as my heart ached towards Ma. He was taking too much of her; with his big, brash, demanding manner he left no room for me.

I sloped away, my elation soured. I had won Ma back only to remember that Balx was stealing her from me.

Chapter Two

Outside, it was a bloated autumn day, the air heavy with moisture and heat. Violet clouds piled over the horizon, stark against an oppressive pewter sky. The drone of insects formed a low, continuous undertone. Somewhere a hook-beak screeched a warning call.

I sought my usual seat on the top step of the porch, clear of the rodents and mudbugs that scurried and squirmed on the ground below. The step gave its customary groan as I sat down, a sound I always interpreted as a welcome.

"Good to see you too," I whispered. I leant my head against the railing and wrapped my hand around one of the struts, wiggling my fingernails into the wood. The grain gave way with satisfying ease. Damp, like it always was. Ma had explained this to me once, how the swamps trapped the moisture in the air so that it sank into the house's bones, making it droop like a sweaty old man. I had giggled, thinking of the grey-whiskered elders who gathered in the village square each Salday evening, mopping their foreheads while they argued and wheezed and reminisced.

I released a long breath, letting the sense of familiarity wash over me, and allowed myself to be comforted. Ma was better. After three days of worry and sickness and fright, she was *better*. The miasma hadn't claimed her—she was still alive, and she was still my mother. Who cared about Balx anyway? Ma was going to be all right. That was what mattered.

And I hadn't even had to lie, not really.

"Nereus?"

I jumped. I hadn't heard the door open or close, yet there she was behind me: the mage, Charis Yondarin.

"Mind if I sit with you a moment?"

I nodded stiffly. I didn't like the thought of having her so close to me, but I could hardly refuse when she had just saved Ma's life. Still, I squished up as far as I could against the railings as the mage eased herself down beside me. The step groaned again, shifting its allegiance. I gazed steadfastly into the distance.

"Your Ma will be fine in a few days," the mage said. "A little weak perhaps, but nothing a good rest won't cure."

A fly buzzed ponderously past my nose. I swatted it away. "Ma doesn't like resting."

"It makes no odds if she likes it or not. She has to rest, and rest she will."

The mage sounded exhausted herself. I risked a glance at her. Her long legs were pulled close to her chest and she leaned heavily upon them, hands dangling between her knees. She'd put her gloves back on, thankfully, but even so I could see her fingers were quivering.

I wondered, suddenly, what was happening beneath her mask. I knew all about mages, of course—I'd grown up hearing the rumours and tales of those rare individuals who were immune to the noxious, swamp-bred magic so perilous to the rest of us, and who could turn its power to their own uses. I also knew, roughly, how this came about. Mages were people who'd suffered a terrible exposure to the miasma and yet emerged—somehow—with life and sanity still intact. Where others died or lost themselves to madness, mages gained power instead.

But what happened when a mage healed someone? Did their body immediately neutralise the poison, or were they, for a time, infected again? I eyed the mage's tremulous hands and hunched shoulders. Was she battling the miasma right now?

I dared not ask. Instead I turned away and squinted at the offending swamp. Its fringes began not a hundred yards from where I sat, a straggling line of great, lush leaves, twisting trunks, and magnificent multihued blooms. There was no denying the beauty of that vibrant, burgeoning vegetation, but all the flowers in the world couldn't make me forget the swamp's toxic heart.

"It advances." The mage broke the quiet with soft words.

I swallowed. She was right. When Ma was a girl and Grampa still alive, they could hardly even see the swamp from here, but over the decades it had crept closer. Good farmland had turned to mire, harmless plants warped into deadly flora, and what was once healthy air had become mortal poison.

The miasma was closing in. And, sometime soon, it would reach us.

I didn't want to think about it. I'd only just snatched Ma back from the swamp's grasp; I didn't want to contemplate the possibility of losing my home. I'd always lived in this house, as had Ma, Grampa and Gramma, and their parents before them. The thought of leaving made my chest ache.

But the mage would not drop the subject. "The same thing's happening all over the north," she murmured, half to herself. "Aleus, Evorum, Cartrix… Everywhere the swamp advances, and people sicken." Her sigh was like the rattling of dead leaves.

It struck me that this woman must have witnessed many terrible things in her lifetime. I knew next to nothing compared to her. *Aleus, Evorum, Cartrix.* They might as well have been provinces across the Long Sea for all I knew of them. The shifting swamps made travel difficult, the routes unpredictable. I'd never even been further than the village.

"Will it… Will it ever stop?" I asked, despite myself.

"I don't know." She paused. "I think not."

I shivered. "Then what will we do?"

"Survive," the mage said solemnly. "We will survive. As best we can."

I glanced at her again. She seemed to have recovered a little, sitting up straight with her legs stretched out before her. Her masked face was turned to the swamp.

She did not look at me as she said, "We have not yet discussed the matter of payment."

I bit my lip. I'd almost forgotten about the contract. The mage was right, though—it had to be dealt with. I had spoken the words, promised the price. It had been a risk—Ma and I didn't have much money—but I'd heard that sometimes mages requested only token payments from poorer clients. I hoped that Charis would do the same for us.

"What's your fee?" I asked nervously.

"Nothing you cannot afford."

I clambered up, relieved, ready to fetch Ma's small purse. "Then I'll just—"

"I want the truth."

I halted, one foot upon the step, one upon the porch.

"What?" I said stupidly.

"The truth." The mage swivelled to face me. Her voice was mild, but her dark eyes burned through the mask. "That is all I demand from you, Nereus. The truth. Why did your mother go out in the swamp?"

I gaped at her, horrified by my new predicament. I'd promised to keep Ma's secret, but I had also spoken the ritual, and the contract had been sealed by the mage's power. Even as I stood there hesitating, the tingling warmth rose again in my chest. A subtle nudge, a reminder that I must pay the requested price.

"I… I don't know—" I began, then broke off as the warmth flared into blazing heat. It was as though someone had thrust a candle against my skin—no, *under* my skin. My lie ended in a gasp of pain.

The mage tilted her head. "You cannot lie to me, Nereus. The deal was struck."

My breathing quickened with distress. She had trapped me. I would have to tell her what had happened, or else pay the price with my life. What would she do when she learned the truth? I could not tell with this mysterious woman. She had saved Ma, true, but that didn't mean she could be trusted. Dealing with mages was never straightforward, that much I knew.

"This isn't fair," I whispered.

"On the contrary, Nereus. It's eminently fair. I gave your mother her life, remember?"

I floundered, feeling my chest prickle again. I would have to admit something, or else the contract's magic would erupt.

"It was my fault," I blurted. "I went into the swamp. I… I wanted to play at being a cataphract. And Ma… She came to get me. And she got sick."

I stopped, perspiring but triumphant. That had been the truth. Not the whole truth, but enough to stop the magic working itself on me. Perhaps I would get away without mentioning the helm.

The mage was silent for a moment. Then, "You went to play in the swamp," she repeated. "And your Ma came to fetch you."

I nodded vigorously.

"Then why aren't *you* sick?" The question was soft but intense. "If you were in the swamp, you should be sick too."

I hadn't thought of that. "I… I don't…" Heat gathered in my heart, anticipating my falsehood. I broke off, wincing.

"I would like the whole truth, please, Nereus," the mage said.

My shoulders drooped. I'd been outmanoeuvred. Charis Yondarin was leaching the truth from me as surely as she had leached the poison from my mother.

Sorry, Ma.

"All right," I whispered. "I'll show you."

*

At the back of the house, three water butts stood against the wall. Two were full, brimming after the succession of thunderstorms that had broken overhead almost every summer night. The third was cracked and empty—or so it appeared.

The mage stood to one side, silent and looming, as I prised up the lid of the broken barrel and stood on tiptoe to reach into its depths. I drew aside a piece of old sacking, then my hand met metal. The feel of it, cool and smooth at my fingertips, made me hesitate again. Interfering with the helm had brought me only bad luck so far. Who knew what further misfortune would come from showing it to the mage? But I had no choice, not anymore.

The mage's breath caught as I lifted the helm clear of the barrel—I heard it even through the mesh of her mouth-grille. I turned to her and, heart thudding, gave over my mother's secret.

The mage accepted the helm with exaggerated care. Cradling it in her gloved palms, she held it up to her eye level and turned it this way and that. Her intense scrutiny made me nervous. What was she looking for? There was nothing particularly special about the helm that I could see. It was old and dented and scratched all over, and the filter apparatus was askew—though the seals were still intact. Once, the helm must have been a true sight to behold, polished to a high shine as it adorned the head of a cataphract riding into the swamp to hunt down people turned feral by the miasma. If left unchecked, those malignants would raid settlements on the swamp's fringes, murdering and pillaging. Cataphracts made sure that didn't happen, and their helms kept them safe. This one still worked to protect the wearer from the miasma—I could attest to that—but its heroic gloss was long gone. Its owner must have replaced the helm when its filter got twisted.

To me, it was exciting that the helm had once belonged to a cataphract, but that did not explain what the mage found so fascinating about it. I could only read about cataphracts in my book of hearth-tales that had once belonged to Grampa. When the mage was home at the citadel she must see cataphracts every day, and all of them would have helms that were newer and better than this one. I twisted my fingers together anxiously. I didn't know why Ma kept the helm hidden either, but I suspected that the mage's interest was somehow linked to Ma's secrecy.

"Where did you get this?" the mage breathed.

"It's Ma's," I said uncomfortably.

"And where did she get it?"

"I don't know."

The mage looked at me sharply, but I wasn't evading her this time. The helm was my mother's secret, not mine; I wasn't even supposed to know about it. I had seen it for the first time only two months ago, when I had woken one night to find Ma sneaking out of the bedroom. I'd stayed silent by instinct, sensing the furtive nature of her errand. Pursuing on bare feet, I saw Ma creep round the house and retrieve the helm from its hiding place. I'd watched then, confused and scared, as she donned the headpiece and slipped away from the house. I hadn't dared follow any further and instead cowered in the shadows of the porch as Ma strode out towards the swamp. An eerie phosphorescence rose from that poisonous realm at night, and against its blue-green glow my mother had dwindled to a dark silhouette, then vanished.

That wasn't the only time, either. Since then I had spied Ma sneaking out to the swamp on a score of nights. I had never asked her why. Perhaps I didn't want to hear the answer.

The mage examined the helm for a few moments longer and then handed it back to me. I took it, surprised and suspicious that she'd returned it so easily.

The mage said nothing more as I placed the helm back in the water butt. She was silent too as we walked back round to the front of the house, stepping on planks laid across the mud-slick ground. Only once we were at the porch again did she speak.

"I think," she said conversationally, "that I will stay with you a little longer. Just to make sure that your mother is all right."

I frowned up at her. "I thought you said she just needed to rest."

She shrugged. "Better safe than sorry."

Her nonchalance was obviously feigned. This sudden decision was down to the helm, not Ma's health. But, again, I was powerless. This woman was too clever for me by half. If she wanted to stay she would stay, and there was nothing a ten-year-old boy could do about it.

Chapter Three

As it happened, this development had an unexpected advantage: the mage sent Balx packing, telling him that she would see to Ma's care for the time being. Balx argued, but faced with the mage's cool insistence he eventually surrendered and stomped off down the track. I hung from the porch railings and stuck my tongue out at his retreating back.

With Balx gone, I was finally free to go to Ma's side. I padded to the bedroom and peered in. Ma's head turned towards me. Her eyes were open and clear, purged at last of the miasma's influence.

I bounded over and flung my arms around her. Ma hugged me in return, and although it was not with her usual strength it was still the sweetest thing to feel her embrace tighten around me once more.

"I'm sorry," I whispered into her neck. "I'm really sorry, Ma. It's all my fault. I—"

"Ssh." She pulled me closer. "Ssh, no matter."

"But I—"

She drew me back to look into my face. "Hush, Nereus, hush. It's over. It's done. You've learned your lesson, I can see that. And there's no lasting harm done, is there?" She paused.

"Is there, Nereus?"

I knew what she was asking: whether I had done as I was told, whether the helm was still safe.

I didn't have the courage to tell her it was not.

"No," I said in a small voice. "No lasting harm, Ma."

She hugged me again. "Oh, my boy. You've been so brave. Fetching a mage, striking the contract… You managed so well. Maestress Yondarin tells me she was so impressed that she waived the fee."

"Ma—" I stuttered.

"No more apologies. Please." Her fingers wove into my hair. "Oh, Nereus," she breathed. "When I saw that you were gone, I just couldn't *think*. The idea of losing you…" She inhaled shakily. "My brave boy. I'm so lucky to have you."

I stayed very still in my mother's arms, afraid to move lest the truth of my betrayal slip out of me somehow, like the sweat seeping from my pores.

*

The mage slept on the floor of our front room, hunkered under a blanket. She kept her mask on in my presence, but I still caught the occasional glimpse of bare skin—an ungloved hand, a stretch of ankle—if I came in too early or forgot to announce myself. When this happened I'd duck my head and retreat immediately, though I'd inevitably spend the rest of the day trying unsuccessfully to scour the sight from my mind.

I fretted constantly about the helm. Was it wrong for Ma to have it? Would it get her into trouble? Perhaps the mage was just waiting to gather more information so that she could report Ma to the Council that presided in the citadel.

Perhaps Ma would be arrested. Perhaps *I'd* be arrested. Perhaps they'd drag us away to gaol while the mage stood watching on our porch, mute and expressionless. I itched to pour out my worries to Ma—to explain what had happened, that Charis Yondarin knew what was hidden in our broken water butt—but each time I opened my mouth to tell her, shame stifled the words. So I suffered on alone. By day I did my best to conceal my anxiety, throwing myself into my chores to distract myself—though it didn't help that the mage's mount was tethered beside our smoking shed. I was a little in awe of the huge reptile with its dirty-grey scales, great clawed feet, and long, sinuous neck. Still, there was something horribly disconcerting about the way it fixed me with its slit-eyed stare every time I passed, especially as I was usually lugging a pail of freshly gutted frogs and snakes. I wondered whether the reptile minded the smell of its smaller cousins' flesh curing within the shed. It never appeared distressed, but then what did I know about reptile behaviour? The beast was as unfathomable as its mistress.

If the days were a struggle, the nights were harder. Without work to preoccupy me all my fears rose to the fore, pressing in with the cloying darkness. My dreams filled with faceless figures and dark insidious tendrils. It was an effort to lie still and not give myself away by tossing and turning.

Ma, however, was clearly benefitting from the mage's continued company, for Charis Yondarin turned out to be a vigilant and tender nurse. It took me by surprise. If I was right that the mage was only staying to pry into Ma's secrets, then she was putting a remarkable effort into maintaining her pretext. For the first three days she returned to Ma's bedside every half-wick to check for lingering symptoms. On the following three, she helped each morning to move my mother out of bed, supporting her as she walked gingerly to her chair in the front room. Anything Ma wanted, she fetched; any small complaint she investigated without delay. She even took it upon herself to help me with the traps and the vegetable patch, and to prepare our morning and evening meals.

On the seventh day, even Ma began to protest. "This is all too much," she said as the mage served our breakfast, brimming bowls of spiced oats. I slurped at mine surreptitiously, unwilling to admit that it was delicious. "You must return to the citadel, surely, Maestress. You have more important things to attend to."

Yondarin shook her head. "It is a mage's duty to ensure the wellbeing of any citizens affected by the miasma." She handed Ma a spoon.

"But we have nothing to pay—"

"Do not concern yourself about that. Nereus and I came to an agreement." She nodded to me. "Didn't we?"

I glowered into my bowl.

"It is too good of you," Ma murmured.

The mage made a dismissive gesture. "Eat," she said. "You still need to build your strength." She picked up her own portion and turned to leave; she never ate in our presence.

Ma caught her hand. The mage started, jerking away from the touch. Her bowl clattered to the floor. Oatmeal oozed onto the rug.

Ma drew back. "Oh, I'm sorry. I—"

"No." The mage snatched up a kitchen rag and bent to right the mess. Her breath whistled through her mouth-grille. "It is I who should apologise. I am not… not accustomed to…" She shrugged awkwardly. "It is not often that others initiate… contact."

Ma's expression went strange, both hard and wobbly at the same time. "I only meant to thank you. I did not mean to cause offence."

"I was not offended. Only surprised."

The mage was busying herself with the spilled food, mopping the oats back into the bowl. Ma reached down and, slowly, deliberately, stilled one of her hands. The mage stiffened, but this time she did not pull away.

Ma folded her fingers around the mage's glove. "Thank you, Charis," she said softly.

The mage looked up into Ma's eyes. When she replied, her voice held a trace of wonderment. "You are welcome. Lya."

I watched the adults over the rim of my bowl, dismayed to see Ma so grateful towards our guest. *Don't trust her!* I wanted to yell. *It's not what you think. She isn't here to help.* Yet even as the thought sprang to my mind, I questioned it. There was no denying that Charis Yondarin had saved Ma's life, and that Ma continued to grow stronger under her care. Surely the mage wouldn't have bothered to help so much if she was only after information. But still, I couldn't forget the intensity with which she'd examined the helm. No. I was right—I must be. Charis Yondarin had a darker purpose here, which Ma did not suspect.

Not that my mother was altogether easy with the mage's extended stay. Occasionally, with the excuse of 'giving us some time together', Charis would go out walking, and at these times Ma grew jittery and fretful. She'd ask me to help her to the window, and from there we would observe the tall, dark figure picking her way along the edge of the swamp. Ma's fingers tightened on the sill as, in the distance, the mage waded through the thick flora. The sight set my own stomach curdling in dread amazement. Charis ventured closer to the swamp than anyone else would dare without protection—anyone but a mage, that was. At times she even vanished entirely into the treeline, something that sent Ma grasping for my shoulder, face blanched.

I had no idea what Ma was so scared of, only that it must have something to do with her own covert journeys into the swamp. Once, I worked up the courage to ask.

"Ma, why are you—"

"Ssh," she hissed. "She's coming back. Help me to the chair, quick now."

I looked; the mage was indeed returning. Nevertheless the interruption had been too abrupt. There was something Ma did not want to tell me.

As I eased her back into her seat, I felt the secrets massing around me, thick and close as the autumn air.

Chapter Four

In the evenings, we all three sat together in the front room. Ma would busy herself with some household task, mending a snake trap or putting the finishing touches on one of her baskets. At first the mage had objected, warning Ma that she'd strain herself, but Ma insisted. "If anything will make me feel worse, it's doing nothing all day," she told Charis. "Idleness doesn't agree with me." Eventually the mage had conceded, though only on the condition that she be allowed to help. They talked in low voices or not at all, sitting opposite one another on the old varnished chairs that Gramma and Grampa had made, heads bent over their work. Normally I would have volunteered to help Ma too, or else asked her to recite a rhyme or a tale, but with the mage there I was too shy. Instead I sat on the rug and fidgeted. I wished I could go out on the porch, but during this season it wasn't wise to open the shutters after dark if you had so much as a candle lit; the night air was alive with insects that would swarm in and thump themselves against the lamps or frazzle themselves in the flames. Even with the shutters closed, some dawdle-moths would inevitably wriggle inside to flutter dazedly around the room.

Sometimes I entertained myself by flicking the bugs away

from my lamp, but there was only so much fun to be had with dawdle-moths—they were too slow for the game to be much of a challenge. So when I bored of that, I would get up and fetch my storybook. Bought from a tinker by my Grampa one long-ago summer, it shared a shelf with Ma's slim accounting books, a dusty Scripture, and the patched ABC from which I'd learned my letters. The storybook was by far the most impressive of the lot. No one else in the village had anything like it. A handsome if rather battered volume, it was bound in leather, with large, elaborate illustrations. The paper was thick and creamy, satisfying to handle. I liked to lie on my belly with the book before me and leaf through the pages, though I hurriedly bypassed any tales that featured mages. Once it had given me a horrified thrill to see the pictures of their mysterious masks and black-as-black eyes, but since Charis arrived I'd quickly lost my taste for them. Instead I settled on stories I knew I enjoyed, like that of Sir Merrun, who had single-handedly saved an entire town from an attack by a horde of croftsmen driven mad by the miasma. There was a full-colour woodcut on the tale's title page. Sir Merrun rode a red-scaled reptile and had a red helm and armour to match.

"So you like cataphracts?"

I blinked, startled out of the story. The mage had swivelled in her chair to face me, leaning forward with her arms resting on her thighs.

I shrugged, resenting the interruption.

"Nereus." Ma spoke from her chair. "Don't be rude."

I sighed. "I suppose."

The mage nodded to my book. "Sir Merrun," she observed. "Is he a favourite of yours?"

"I suppose."

"Nereus…" Ma warned again.

Undeterred, the mage held out a hand. "Can I take a look?"

I stuck out my lip, reluctant, but with Ma watching me I didn't have much choice. I scrambled to my knees and handed the book over.

Charis balanced it carefully in her lap. She smoothed a glove over the illustration and read a few lines of text. "So he saved a village."

"A whole town," I corrected. "All by himself."

"Oh?"

"Everyone thought it was impossible," I told her. "There were loads of malignants, so the townsfolk thought they were doomed. But Sir Merrun tricked the malignants by luring them with food." I forgot to be annoyed with the mage as I warmed to my account. "He filled a big barn with barrels of salted meat that the malignants would smell, but among the meat he also put barrels of flashpowder. Then just as the malignants got to the barn, he set fire to it. Bang! Whoosh!" I threw up my arms. "The malignants were so scared that they ran right back into the swamp, all singed and smoky."

"I see," said the mage. She didn't sound particularly impressed. "So what do you like most about him?"

"He's clever and brave," I said. "And he's got red armour."

"It is very fine armour," she conceded. "Did you know that mages help to make part of a cataphract's armour?"

I was taken aback. "They do?"

"The helms," Charis said. "We make the filters for them. It's done by extracting a part of the miasma, you see, and adapting it so that it neutralises the poison. Only mages can do that, so only mages can make the filters."

I stiffened at the mention of helms, then cast my eyes down

and began picking angrily at the rug. I felt as though I'd been in some way led on.

Behind the mage, Ma shifted in her chair. "I think perhaps—" she began.

"I know a story about a cataphract," the mage said easily, as though she hadn't noticed our reactions. "A story that isn't in your book." She closed the volume. "Would you like to hear it?"

I hesitated, intrigued despite myself. We only had one storybook, and the opportunity to hear more tales didn't come along often. I remembered what Charis Yondarin had said that first day she was here, about all those distant places. She had travelled to so many far-flung parts; she must know lots of exciting stories. "All right," I said.

"I think," said Ma again, "that it's time Nereus went to bed."

"But, Ma," I remonstrated. "I want to hear about the cataphract."

"You know enough stories about cataphracts." Ma's voice had become slightly strained.

Charis glanced at her. "It won't take long."

"I don't know…"

"Please, Ma."

Ma pressed her lips together.

Charis took her silence as consent. "It happened," she began in her muffled, husky voice, "in a village quite far away from here, but not so far away as you might think. It was not a very remarkable place. It had a butcher's and a baker's and a square and a church and some farms and smallholdings and an inn with a big porch where the men liked to slouch about and smoke.

"The people of the village were kind in their way, but they were also stubborn. They had to be, for the village was very isolated, surrounded on three sides by deep swathes of swamp."

I nodded. I didn't need to imagine the type of people Charis meant; I lived among them. Whenever I went into the village, to the market with Ma or to scamper about in the square with the other boys, I encountered the mixture of personality that Charis spoke of: benevolence tempered by obstinacy.

"Every year the swamp crept closer to the village," Charis continued. "Some people left, fearful of the miasma, but most stayed. Even when officials from the citadel came to warn them of the danger, they refused to move. They had lived in the village all their lives, as had their parents, their grandparents and their great-grandparents. They didn't want to leave until it was absolutely necessary."

I nodded again. I understood this too.

"Then, one day, a farmer from the village set out to travel to the town, where he intended to sell his produce. There was only one road he could take to get beyond the village, for all other routes had been swallowed by the swamp long ago. But as he drove his cart along, he found that the swamp had now oozed across the road so that there was no way through.

"The farmer rushed back to the village to tell the Patron. The Patron was very alarmed, and at once sent riders out in every direction to see if any of the old thoroughfares had opened up with the swamp's shifting. But none had. The village was now surrounded on all sides. They were trapped."

I hugged my knees, thrilled and fascinated. I'd definitely never heard this story before. "What did they do?"

Charis regarded me gravely. "What could they do? There was no way for them to get through. There were no mages or cataphracts in the village who could travel safely through the miasma to fetch help. They didn't even have any reptiles so that they could try to ride through quickly without being overcome. The only steeds they had were asses and the Patron's horse."

"They could send birds," I said, proud of my reasoning. "Birds don't get sick."

"They were unlucky there, too. For the Patron was the only person who owned any birds, and his had been attacked by a buzzhawk last time they went out and could no longer fly." Charis spread her hands. "They had no way at all to get a message to the citadel."

"Terrifying." Ma spoke softly from her chair. I looked at her and saw that her weaving lay forgotten on her lap. It seemed she was listening to the story after all.

"Yes," agreed Charis. "The villagers were very frightened. They didn't know whether someone from outside would notice that their road was blocked and come and rescue them. It seemed unlikely, and at any rate they couldn't wait forever, because the swamp was still closing in. A few people decided that the only course of action was to risk their own lives and try to get through the miasma, even though they had no filters to protect themselves and no reptiles to ride."

I thought this very courageous and opened my mouth to say so, but Charis held up a finger.

"While this was certainly brave," she said, "it was also extreme folly. For of course the miasma quickly made them sick, and if they didn't die from the sickness it drove them mad. And then they turned around and started raiding the village, attacking the very people they had set out to save."

"Oh," I said, feeling stupid and rather tense. This story was a bit solemn for my liking. "So what about the cataphract?"

"I haven't got to the cataphract yet."

"Oh," I said again, wishing that the mage would just skip to that part. "So what happened next?"

Charis leaned back in her chair. "The Patron had an idea, though he didn't tell the other villagers about it straight away, because he knew they wouldn't like it. He didn't like it very much either. But rack his brains as he might, he couldn't think of anything else. So the next day he gathered everyone in the village hall.

"'The swamp is getting closer,' he said. 'It's almost on our doorsteps. We can't wait for rescue any longer. There isn't time.'

"'But what else can we do?' the villagers asked. 'We've tried everything. Our only chance is to pray to the Hale that the Council hears about our plight and sends a cataphract and a mage to save us.'

"'Or,' said the Patron, 'we could make our own mage.'

"The villagers were confused, but the Patron explained. If someone went into the swamp and, instead of dying or going mad, became a mage, then they could take a message to the outside world, then return and help make filters to lead the people to safety.

"'But it's so rare for someone to become a mage,' the villagers protested. 'You can't predict it. Just look at the people who've already tried to get through the swamp. None of them turned into mages.'

"'That's because they were too old,' said the Patron. 'You know what the scholars say—you're much more likely to become a mage when you're young.'

"Everyone in the hall went very quiet. Suddenly they understood what the Patron was suggesting. That they should send their children out into the swamp to see if they would survive to become mages."

My mouth hung open. "No," I whispered. "They didn't!"

The mage shrugged, horribly nonchalant. "They were desperate. They didn't think they had another choice. So they rounded up the strongest of the children and forced them into the swamp. The children screamed and cried and the parents cried too, but still they did it."

"The children stayed near the edge of the swamp at first, and every so often they tried to run back into the village, but the adults who had once been their friends and families drove them back in. So they wandered about and soon got lost. Some fell into sinkholes which sucked them in and stuck them fast. Some were attacked by strange, scaly beasts that uncurled from between the roots of trees. Some simply sat upon the ground and hid their faces in their hands. And all the while they were getting sick. The miasma oozed from the plants and the soil and they couldn't help but breathe it in. The poison raced through their blood and made them feverish. They coughed and spluttered and sneezed. Their bodies changed; their blood darkened. Some died very quickly, some slowly, and those who didn't die instead began to rave and screech. Their cries were audible from the village. The villagers wept to hear them, but they were convinced that this was their only chance at survival."

I shivered despite the evening's warmth. Charis's tale was not turning out like I'd expected. The cataphract hadn't even been mentioned; it was all about the cowardly villagers and their unfortunate children. I couldn't even work out whom to root for. In this story, you couldn't even hate the malignants. In the tale of Sir Merrun, the malignants were all grown-ups who had gone into the swamp because they were greedy and stupid, so you knew that they were bad and Sir Merrun was good. Charis's account wasn't like that.

Besides, her description of the children's fate in the swamp had made me feel a little giddy. When I had taken the helm, I had only ventured a tiny way into the swamp, just to see what it was like, to feel I was being brave like a cataphract. Now the thought of what I'd done set goosepimples rising on my arms. I looked at Ma and was unnerved still more when I saw tears blurring her eyes.

Charis spoke on. "Little did the villagers know that someone had indeed noticed their plight. In the town, the marketkeepers thought it strange that no one from the village had come to trade. They reported their concerns to the Council, who immediately sent a cataphract and a mage to investigate."

I perked up. "A cataphract!" At last. Maybe the story would get better now.

"That's right. He and the mage travelled as quickly as they could to the village, riding their reptiles through the swamp. But when they arrived, they found the village under attack. The children who had survived the miasma had lost their minds. They growled and clawed and leapt like beasts. Returning to their former homes, they were sneaking into the village for food and fighting anyone who got in their way."

I grimaced. "But the cataphract saved the village?" I asked, eager for a resolution to this troubling tale.

Charis inclined her head. "He did."

I was tentatively relieved. "He drove away the children?"

"He killed the children."

"He…" I stumbled over the words. "He killed them?"

"As far as the cataphract was concerned, it was his duty to make the village safe again. He charged in with his sword swinging. The children fled before him, so he chased them on his reptile and hunted them down one by one."

"But that's not—" I began.

The mage was not finished. "When the swamp was finally quiet and there were no more cries of malignants, the cataphract stopped in a clearing near the edge of the swamp. There he dismounted and cleaned the blood from his sword, because he knew the villagers would be even more upset if he emerged with a dripping blade. But as he cleaned his weapon, there came a rustling from behind him. The cataphract span round and saw a girl emerge from the bushes. She was very dirty, but he could see that she was marked like the other children had been.

"The girl raised her hands and stepped towards the cataphract, but before she could come any closer the cataphract stabbed her with his sword. One quick jab, in and out." I flinched as Charis pumped her arm, miming the thrust. "The girl clutched at the wound and ran bleeding into the swamp. The cataphract did not bother to follow her. He had given her a grievous blow and knew that she would die from her injury."

Charis paused, then plunged on in a falsely cheerful tone. "And so the village was delivered. The mage made filters for the trapped villagers that they could tie around their noses and mouths, and once they were all attired the cataphract led them through the swamp and out, at last, to safety."

In the ensuing silence, a dawdle-moth flopped repeatedly against my reading lamp. Its furry body made dull thunks on the glass.

Eventually I asked, "How did the cataphract know?"

"Know what, Nereus?"

I licked my lips. They had gone very dry. "How did he know that the girl was malignant? How did he know she wasn't a mage?"

Charis regarded me. "He didn't."

"But… But…" I didn't understand. That was not the way cataphracts were supposed to behave. They were noble and gracious. They swore oaths to protect the hale—and even mages were hale, in their way. They weren't malignants, at any rate. "He wasn't a proper cataphract," I concluded, taking refuge in scorn.

"You would be surprised how many cataphracts have similar stories," said Charis, "were there anyone left to recount them."

I decided not to believe her. "What was his name?" I asked, determined never to hear any stories about this imposter again.

"Sir Gildas," said Charis. "His name was Sir Gildas."

"Well, I think he was a bad cataphract," I said stoutly. "Ma, don't you reckon he wasn't a proper… Ma?"

Ma was sitting frozen in her chair, and even in the lamplight's yellow glow I could see that she had turned very pale. Her weaving slid from her lap to crumple on the floor. Ma ignored it. She was staring at the mage.

Charis Yondarin gazed levelly back.

I looked from one to the other, bewildered. "Ma?"

"Lya," said the mage. "Why don't you tell me about the helm?"

I jumped up. "Ma!" I gasped. "It's not my fault! She tricked me!" I stumbled over and clutched my mother's skirts. "The contract—I had to!"

Ma shushed me with a hand on my wrist. "It's all right,

Nereus," she said, though she didn't sound too certain; her words were more question than statement. "You can leave us."

"What? But—"

"Please. Go on to bed." Her eyes remained locked with the mage's even as she spoke to me.

"But I—"

"Go."

I relinquished my grip on her skirts and dragged my feet to the door of the bedroom. It was torture to be ordered away when I was aching to know what was going to happen, and scared for Ma besides. But I knew that nothing could sway Ma when she used that tone.

I meant to go to bed like Ma had asked—I really did—but once I'd shut the bedroom door behind me I couldn't bear to lie down; there were too many questions and worries bouncing around my head. Instead, I knelt and put my eye to the crack between door and frame and squinted through. To my dismay, all I could see were the backs of the adults' heads as they leaned close together, and all I could hear of their talk were indecipherable murmurs.

Their discussion lasted many wicks. I sat by the door on the hard floor, trying periodically to spy again, but each attempt was as fruitless as the first.

Sleep came fitfully, fretfully. Every so often I dozed, only to start awake and peep through the crack again, then slump back and doze a little more. The events of the night merged and stretched, becoming hazy and dreamlike. At one point, peering into the front room, I thought I saw the mage's mask discarded on the floorboards and Ma's hand—picked out by the guttering lamplight—reaching to touch something beyond my line of sight. Another time I looked in only to find the room filled with plants, a dense jungle of vines and creepers tangling over the chairs and table. Our jackets, burst at the seams, were held aloft upon curling stems. Stalks punctured the rug to reach up to the ceiling. My storybook hung in tatters, its pages transformed into vast green leaves. Half-buried in loam, a metallic gleam hinted at the helm's presence. And there, from the shadows in the midst of the chaos, a pair of eyes stared back at me, dark and unblinking.

Chapter Five

I awoke curled beside the door, stiff from sleeping on the hard floorboards. The shutters were closed, but shafts of daylight had pushed their way through to spear across the room, striping the wall. Outside, swellfrogs and razorbugs raised their grating morning chorus, croaking and burring their indignation at the sun.

I felt like doing the same as I clambered to my feet, rubbing grit from my eyes. Why had Ma let me sleep on the floor? It was only then, as I looked accusingly towards the bed, that I realised it was empty. The pillows were undented, the sheets tucked pristinely round the pallet. Ma hadn't been in all night.

For a few moments I stood in a daze, staring at the untouched bedclothes. Then, like a bent twig flicking back into place, the events of the evening sprang into my mind. I remembered the muggy room, the mage's tale, Ma's shock. I remembered Charis's question about the helm. But after that, everything grew hazy.

Panic seized me. What had happened while I slept? Had the mage spirited Ma away? Taken her as a prisoner back to the Council? Or even, Hale forbid, punished her?

I burst into the front room only to find it as deserted as

the bedroom. Nothing appeared disturbed. The same faded rug still lay upon the floor; the same table still stood upon it with the same chairs tucked beneath. The same shelves lined the walls, crowded with the same assortment of jars, pans, and household knick-knacks. The same iron stove crouched, pot-bellied, in the corner. The familiar objects should have been comforting, but instead they seemed somehow sinister. It was as though they knew something I didn't, and in the knowing of it they had become co-conspirators against me.

My fear intensified. Racing across the room, I threw the front door open and clattered outside, only to skid to a halt when I nearly blundered into the mage. She was sitting on the porch step—*my* step—her masked head bent over something in her lap.

She looked up as I teetered above her. "Good morning, Nereus. Is something wrong?"

"Where's Ma?" I demanded. "Where is she?"

Charis did not react to my urgency. "Your mother is over there." She pointed out beyond the porch. I followed her gesture and, with a surge of relief, spotted Ma a little way off. She had squelched out across the muddy ground into the thick grasses beyond the track and now stood with her back to the house, facing the swamp. Her posture was very still and very straight. With the towering trees of the swamp before her, she resembled a lone warrior facing down an army of gigantic, alien foes.

I started down the steps, but the mage took hold of my arm. "Wait," she cautioned. "She is thinking. I doubt she wants to be disturbed."

I struggled. "Let go!" I cried.

She did so immediately, yet her words had done their work.

I dithered on the steps. As much as I wanted to run to Ma, I had to admit that the mage was right—Ma did look lost in thought. But why? What was this all about? Now I knew Ma was safe, that was what I ached to find out.

My frustration got the better of me. "What happened?" I burst out. "What did you talk about last night? Why does Ma have that helm?"

Charis shook her head. "I'm afraid it is not my place to answer those questions. I must leave that to your mother, when she is ready."

I rocked on the balls of my feet. "Are we in trouble though?"

"Not from me."

Reluctantly, I sank down to sit on the step. Seeing that I was calmer, the mage returned her attention to the thing in her lap. I frowned at it too, taking more notice now that my panic had subsided. Once again, I found myself confused. The mage had collected some strips of sackcloth and a broken leather belt, which she was stitching together to form a kind of sling.

"What's that for?" I asked.

"You'll see when it's finished." Her black eyes flickered to Ma, and she shrugged. "Or maybe it will be for nothing at all."

Her evasion exasperated me. I crossed my arms over my knees. "No one tells me anything," I muttered.

The mage eyed me as she continued stitching. "What is it you wish to know?"

"Everything!" I bit off my outburst, sought for a more grown-up answer. Remembering the mage's original demand of me, I echoed it. "The truth," I said.

"The truth will not always be to your liking."

I bridled. "I don't care."

The mage put down her work. When she looked at me next, her gaze was fierce. "You want truth, Nereus? I can show you something true. But I warn you now, you will have to be brave."

I gulped. Despite my bravado, I knew I was not courageous. Ma was tough, tough as a woman had to be to live out here at the swamp's edge with only her young son for company. Plenty of people had tried to persuade her to move to the village proper—Balx had been particularly vocal on this point—but she had always declined. She managed well enough out here, she told them. And she did.

I, on the other hand, relied entirely upon her. And it wasn't just because of my age. I was painfully aware that I didn't have the same mettle as my mother. It was the real reason I had borrowed the helm in the first place, to prove to myself that I was brave enough to put it on and venture into the swamp like Ma did. But the adventure had proved nothing except that I was a fool. I had only terrified myself and almost killed Ma in the process. No, I was not like my mother. I was too much of a coward.

Yet here was Charis Yondarin, telling me that the price of knowledge was bravery. If I wanted to unlock the secrets that surrounded me, I had to confront my fears.

"Well, Nereus? Are you ready?"

I forced myself to stop hugging my legs and sat up straight. "Yes," I said.

Charis nodded gravely, as though we had just struck another of her binding contracts. Then she began unbuttoning her jerkin.

My pulse quickened in horror, but somehow I managed to keep my seat as Charis slowly revealed her affected flesh. I looked aside instinctively, then remembered that this was what I had asked for. This was what I had wanted.

Be brave. I repeated the mage's words like a mantra. *You will have to be brave.* Steeling myself, I turned my eyes back to Charis.

It was not as terrible as I had imagined. A hardened patch of skin—like on the back of her hand—curled around Charis's neckline and across one shoulder. It was the muddy green of brackish water, speckled with knobbly scutes like a bird's leg. Crawling out from beneath it were more black veins, which spread across her upper chest before disappearing beneath the wrap she wore around her breasts. Aside from this, however, Charis's body had the same foibles as anyone's. Or so I thought, until the mage pulled open the left side of her tunic to expose a long scar.

At first I thought it was another remnant of the miasma, a symptom I'd never heard about before, but quickly realised my mistake. Livid white, the scar struck a neat line diagonally across her abdomen. No disease could have left such a mark. The cut must have been made by something sharp and precise. Like a sword.

My mouth fell open. "That was *you*?"

"That was me."

"But I thought it was a story!"

Calmly, Charis rebuttoned her tunic. "It was," she said. "It was my story."

I sat silent, taking this in. Guilt wound tendrils around me as I thought about how I'd treated the mage with such revulsion. It wasn't her fault she looked so scary. She had been forced defenceless into the miasma by her own family, the very people who were supposed to protect her. Whereas Ma had risked her life in the swamp to find me, Charis's parents had thrown their daughter in to save themselves. And then, after all she had been through—the agonies of sickness, the torment of watching other children dying around her—she had emerged only to be attacked by a cataphract, a man who was meant to be a hero.

How had she survived? I burned to ask more, but before I could voice my questions the mage spoke again.

"Your mother is returning."

I scrambled to my feet as Ma approached the porch and halted at the base of the steps.

"Nereus." She held out her hands. Her expression was determined and also a little beseeching, as though she had come to a decision but was nevertheless in need of comfort.

I went to her.

Ma crouched to look me in the eyes. "Nereus," she said again. "Nereus, my brave boy." Her grip tightened on my hands; I felt the calluses across her palms. "Tell me… How would you like to meet your sister?"

Sister? I didn't have a sister. I stared at Ma, but there was no trace of a joke in her manner. After a moment I turned to the mage, as if she could offer some solution to my bafflement, and saw that Charis had also risen to her feet. She was holding the strange thing she'd been making, and suddenly I realised what it was. The belt would strap around someone's head, while the sackcloth would cover their nose and mouth.

A filter. The mage was making another filter.

And that could mean only one thing.

Chapter Six

I'd been seven years old when I declared myself too old for handholding, disentangling my fingers from Ma's on the way to the schoolroom one morning and then sneaking a look at the village children to make sure they'd noticed my bold move. But today, as we picked our way towards the swamp, I found Ma's hand and clung to it as tightly as though I were a little kid again.

Ahead of us loomed the great wall of foliage, reminding me of the crenellated walls that surrounded the citadel in the illustrations of my storybook. The ground grew more treacherous the closer we came, riddled with tussocks that tripped me up at every other step and thick with mud that slurped hungrily at my boots. I was sweltering in my outfit too. The metal helm was heavy and hot, and my neck chafed where the gorget was sealed tight against my skin. Ma had also insisted that I wear my thickest jacket buttoned up to the chin, along with my heavy work gloves. The miasma was not infectious merely upon contact with skin, but open wounds could be dangerous and she didn't want me taking any chances. Ma herself wore the new filter made by the mage, tied snugly around her nose and mouth, and hardy clothing like my own—the same garments she wore when she sneaked out at night.

I now knew the reason for those midnight excursions, though it still made my head spin to think of it. When Ma had explained it to me—as she helped me dress for our expedition—I could only stand mute, listening in shock.

I had a sister, Ma had told me in a solemn voice. I had a sister whom I'd never met. Her name was Hagne. Six years my elder, Hagne had lived here before I was born. She had played on the same porch as I did, lounged on the same rug, slept in the same bed, even read the same book of tales.

This was all when my father was here. I had never met him either. On the rare occasions he was mentioned, Ma's expression would close like a withering flower and her shoulders hunch defensively. I hated to see her upset, so I'd seldom brought up the topic of the man who'd sired me. Before now, all I'd known of him was that he had left my mother shortly before I was born, and that this, as far as Ma was concerned, had been a lucky escape for both of us. I'd never missed him especially, never even wished that I'd known him. Ma had always been enough for me.

As she buttoned up my jacket, Ma revealed that my father had been a hard man. More than that, he had been a bully. It hadn't been that way at first, when they married and he moved out here to live with Ma (his family, like many others, had been uprooted by the shifting swamps). Back then, his curt, practical nature had been a boon, and a good match for his wife's pragmatism. But as the years passed and the swamp expanded its margins inch by inch, my father's temper had swelled along with it. Terse words turned to insults; insults became tirades; tirades escalated into outright rages. By the time Hagne was three, showers of smashed crockery were commonplace. By the time she was five, she and Ma lived under the constant threat of blows. Soon, Ma and Hagne were more afraid of my father than of the swamp itself. The poison in their own home had grown more toxic than that which approached outside.

My sister was only six on the night she fled the house, her back still striped with welts from our father's belt.

The following morning, Ma had found her daughter's bed empty.

Recounting this moment, Ma's fingers shook so much that she could no longer do up my buttons. "I couldn't protect her," she whispered. "I couldn't keep my child safe. I looked for her everywhere, everywhere I could think of, everywhere except…" She gave up on the buttons and clutched the fabric of my jacket. "I would have followed her there too," she told me fiercely. "I would. But you were already inside me by that time and I couldn't risk you as well. I begged your father to go in and search for her, but back then we didn't have the helm to protect us and he refused to go. He said she'd realise her mistake soon enough. He said she would come back." Ma gave a hollow, haunted laugh. "He was right, in a way. Hagne did come back. But she wasn't… wasn't the same." Ma's hands began to shake again, and her voice choked. "I couldn't call a cataphract, Nereus. I just couldn't."

I stood wide-eyed, trying to take it all in. "You look after her," I said wonderingly. "That's where you go at night."

Ma nodded.

"But isn't she…" I hesitated. I didn't want to add to Ma's distress, but I couldn't think of a better way to put it. "Isn't she… mad?"

Ma wiped her eyes on her sleeve, composing herself. "You will see what she is." She handed me my gloves and kissed my forehead. "You mustn't be afraid."

I tried to follow Ma's instruction as we reached the edge of the swamp, but no matter what I did I couldn't stop my heart pounding as we pushed our way into the foliage.

Entering the swamp was like trespassing into another world. The heat increased almost immediately as the vegetation engulfed us and a sudden hush fell, as though a blanket had been draped over everything. I wrinkled my nose. Even through the helm's filter I could detect a strange odour: pungent and loamy, yet laced with a sharper, acidic note. I tried not to think about what it might be.

Our progress slowed. Ma went first with me in tow, Charis following behind. At every step dense shrubs and grasses tugged at our breeches and our boots sank into thick black mulch. At times the soil gave way to oozing, sludge-topped waterways, over which we had to jump or else skirt the edge until we found a way across. Around us, vine-bedecked tree trunks rose to twine and tangle above our heads, blocking out the daylight so that we moved through an aquatic gloom. Leaves clustered close on all sides, ranging in size from tiny feathery points to gigantic rubbery fronds with veins that visibly pulsed with life. The flowers too were monstrous in their vigour, their colours so riotous they hurt my eyes. Sprays of pollen showered from the bulbous blooms as we brushed past, and overgrown insects hummed past our ears as they leapt suddenly from swaying stalks. Other earthbound bugs hurried away from us, some with long, swollen bodies that undulated along the ground, others on articulated legs that clicked audibly as they went. I avoided the insects only to step instead on fallen seedpods that burst wetly beneath my weight, spilling tiny granules upon the mud. Occasionally a ripple in the undergrowth hinted at other, larger creatures skittering past.

I realised I was holding my breath and had to force myself to let it out. *Don't be a baby*, I scolded myself. *You've got the helm on. The miasma can't hurt you.* Besides, this wasn't even the first time I'd been in the swamp. I thought back to that disastrous morning when I'd taken the helm to play cataphract. I'd been alone then, too. That had been different, though—I'd been so excited at my own daring that I'd forgotten the extent of my peril. Now, with the grisly descriptions from Charis's tale fresh in my mind, the swamp's dangers were frighteningly clear to me. No matter what I told myself, I couldn't help but flinch away from bobbing flower-heads, wince at the crunch of seedpods, and shiver at the fungi that formed rainbow-hued stairways round the trunks of trees.

And my sister… what about her? Hadn't the miasma driven her out of her wits? Surely she would attack us, like the children from Charis's village had attacked their families?

No. I gritted my teeth. *It will be all right. Ma said so.*

I'd lost track of how far we'd come by the time Ma halted. She brought us to a stop in a small clearing where the ground was relatively firm. In the centre was a tree whose slanting trunk was mottled with thick, blueish moss. A hefty bough stood out from its side, and from it dripped a curtain of tendril-like growths that might have been flowers, or fungi, or something in between. Ma drew the growths aside, revealing something hidden among them. I blinked in surprise. It was a small kitchen pan, battered and rusting, looking entirely out of place where it hung from the bough by a length of twine. Taking a stick from the ground, Ma struck the pan three times. The metal clanged with each blow, yet the noise was cut oddly short, absorbed by the surrounding swamp. It seemed impossible that the sound would be heard any distance away. It occurred to me that this must be why I had not heard Ma calling to me that morning when she'd come searching for me in the swamp.

Ma, however, seemed confident that my sister would appear, and stood watching our surroundings intently. I fidgeted beside her, becoming more and more nervous.

"Ma," I whispered after a while, my voice beneath the helm sounding tinny in my ears, "I don't think—"

A rustling to our right cut me off. I pressed closer to Ma, but the noise stopped as abruptly as it had started. Heart racing, I peered in the direction it had come from, but there was no further sound and no movement either. No sister emerged from the gloom.

"She's not used to anyone but me," Ma said. Moving forward, she tried to extricate her hand from mine.

I didn't let her.

"Nereus, please." Ma glanced down at me. Her face looked strange with the filter strapped around it—like a frog, or a bug. "Let go. Just for a little while."

I shook my head. I didn't want to lose contact with Ma. I didn't want to feel alone out here.

Charis stepped up behind me. The mage put a hand on my shoulder and squeezed. "It's all right. Your mother isn't going anywhere."

Not so long ago, the mage's touch would have set me flinching. Now, however, I found that Charis's presence was a comfort. The mage was accustomed to the swamp's tricks and had no problems negotiating its treacherous terrain. She knew this place, had been transformed by this place, and if something went wrong she could always scour the miasma from our blood.

But her usefulness wasn't the only reason I felt reassured by Charis. No, it ran deeper than that. I realised then that I had come to trust her.

Slowly, I released Ma's hand. Charis gave my shoulder another squeeze. "Well done," she murmured.

Ma stepped away and called softly. "Hagne? Are you there? Hagne?"

She paused. After a moment another rustle sounded, this time from our left. I shrank towards Charis, grateful to have her at my back. If that rustling was caused by my sister, she must have moved around the clearing's edge with unnatural silence.

Ma was unperturbed. Turning towards the noise, she called again. "Come on out, Hagne. I've brought someone for you to meet."

Still no one appeared. I worried my lip beneath the helm. All this waiting was making me feel a little sick.

Now Ma also seemed to be growing anxious, her posture stiffening as she scanned the jungle around us. Despite this, she kept her tone soothing as she tried calling my sister once more. "It's all right, Hagne. They're friends, I promise. No one is here to hurt you."

No response. After peering about for a minute longer, Ma's shoulders finally slumped. She plodded back to us. "Perhaps this wasn't a good idea," she admitted.

Charis stepped forward. "May I try?"

Ma looked taken aback, but she nodded. "Of course. Though I'm not sure she will come. I thought she would be ready to meet you, but..."

"We will see," Charis said. She moved past Ma and stood looking out at the undergrowth, gloved hands resting on her slim hips. Then she did an unexpected thing. Reaching up, she unfastened the buckles at her neck, releasing the straps that held her mask in place. The hood peeled open along the back of her head, its leather sides unfurling like the petals of a mootbloom. Charis eased it off to reveal her discoloured scalp, ill-hidden by her cropped, patchy hair.

The first time I had seen the mage unmasked, I had fled. This time I stood my ground. I knew Charis now. I had learnt that her disturbing appearance did not reflect her character. She was reliable and caring, kind to Ma and kind to me. The least I could do in return was to accept her as she was.

Head bare, Charis bowed deeply to the silent swamp.

"Greetings, Hagne," she said. "My name is Charis Yondarin. It would be an honour to make your acquaintance. Will you come out to meet us?"

At first the quiet continued, and I thought that Charis's effort would be for nothing. Then a flash of movement from above caught my attention. I span round—Ma and Charis with me—just in time to see a figure vault down from the tree, dropping from its outflung branch to land in a crouch.

My first sighting of my sister was a confused impression of thin, gangly limbs, matted strings of hair, a sallow face, and the glint of a shrewd eye. That was all I could take in before she was in motion again, bounding towards the mage. It was only when she halted before Charis and peered into the mage's face that I was able to examine her properly.

Seeing Hagne and Charis together, I immediately noticed their similarity. The miasma had mercilessly carved its mark into each countenance, leaving in its wake the disfigurations that would always brand them as victims of the swamp. Like Charis, my sister's skin was piebald, hardened blotches of green and grey speckling her paleness. Black veins crawled across her features, and her lips and irises were dark as well. What hair she had was brittle-looking and matted.

Yet Hagne did not only resemble Charis. Despite everything my sister had endured, I could see in her face the shadow of Ma's features. And not just Ma's. With that narrow face and stubby nose, she also looked a lot like me. The realisation brought a lump to my throat, though I couldn't tell whether what I was feeling was happiness or shock.

My sister inspected Charis's face for a few moments longer, frowning. Then she leapt away again, landing on all fours to scamper back under the tree and then stand, half-hidden by the curtain of hanging growths. I bit back a yelp of surprise. Each motion Hagne made was so swift, so abrupt, that it made me jump. Her agility seemed more animal than human. It was as though she'd decided that merely walking on two legs was stupid and boring compared to the darting of reptiles, the twitching of birds, and the scuttling of insects.

But wasn't that true? My gaze wandered, taking in anew the tangled and treacherous place in which we stood. Whereas I had struggled my way through the sludge and the plants, my sister swept through the swamp light-footed and spry. I was helpless in here compared to her. It was almost as though she were a different order of being.

But not quite. Standing beneath the tree, Hagne was peeking shyly through the hanging plants, twisting one bare toe in the dirt. Ma must have given her clothes at some point, for she wore a shift and leggings, though the garments were torn and soiled. She played with the fraying lacings of her shift as she regarded us. Her mannerisms were instantly familiar. I'd seen the village girls act the same way as they hid behind the water-pump and watched the boys playing Get-Um in the square.

"Hagne," Ma said. "There you are." She unslung a bundle from her back, which I now realised must contain food and other supplies, and pressed it into my hands. "Here, Nereus. You can give it to her this time."

I stared at the bundle, suddenly terrified. My sister had been friendly enough so far, but how did I know it would last? I scrutinised her again. She examined me in return. When her gaze lighted on the parcel, her lips parted eagerly. Apart from that, it was impossible to tell what she was thinking.

How much did she comprehend? Had she understood Ma's words, or Charis's? Or had she just been attracted by things that were familiar to her: Ma's soothing tones and Charis's swamp-moulded body? I, meanwhile, was a stranger, a scrawny boy in a bizarre metal helmet. Would she behave so gently towards me when I got close to her?

Ma didn't seem to have any doubts. She urged me forward with an arm round my shoulders. "Come on. We'll go together."

Taking a deep breath, I succumbed to Ma's insistence. She would never put me in danger. If Ma said it was all right, it must be.

We advanced. My sister drew back a little, her focus darting between us, her knees bending into a slight crouch. When we were a few feet away, we stopped.

"Hagne?" Ma said gently. "This is Nereus, your little brother. Nereus, this is your sister, Hagne."

Hagne blinked at Ma and then at me.

"Hold out the bundle," Ma whispered in my ear. "Hold it out for her."

I did so, nervously. Hagne regarded the offering with some suspicion. She took a couple of steps forward, venturing out from behind the hanging plants, but then retreated again. I waited, as I knew Ma wanted me to. Hagne glanced at Ma, licking her lips.

"Go on," Ma said. "Take it, Hagne. It's for you."

My sister tiptoed forward again, coming nearer this time. Sidestepping around me, she considered the bundle with her neck extended, like a bird inspecting crumbs strewn upon the ground. This close, her disfigurations were clearly visible, a map of her misfortunes etched onto her face. She smelt strongly of dirt and sweat. She reached out a hand, fingers brushing the bundle. Her nails were long, broken, and blackened too. I suppressed the urge to shrink back, instead concentrating on the weight of Ma's arm across my shoulders, the rhythm of her breaths falling on my cheek.

I stood my ground, but at the last instant Hagne withdrew her hands and fled, returning to her place beneath the tree.

Ma sighed. "All right, Nereus," she murmured. "Just put the bundle down. Just leave it here."

I did as I was told, laying the bundle on the soggy ground. Then Ma and I drew back. As soon as we were far enough away, Hagne scooted forward, snatched up the bundle, and retreated again to a safe distance. There she crouched and rifled through the supplies. There were strips of dried snake-meat and crunchy insects, root vegetables and jars of pickles, a skin of fresh water and a change of clothes. She picked out each offering and inspected it closely, sniffing it and rolling it around in her palms. A joyful sound escaped her, and when she turned her gaze to Ma it was so clearly full of gratitude that for a moment she didn't seem swamp-struck at all, but like any other child who'd been given a much-wanted gift.

Gathering the bundle to her chest, Hagne backed away into the undergrowth. Except, before vanishing, she hesitated. I let out a gasp as she suddenly rushed towards us, sprinting up to Ma to stroke her tenderly on the arm. That done, she turned her face to the swamp and plunged into the dripping gloom.

Ma cleared her throat. "She's not usually so shy," she said apologetically. She patted my shoulder. "Never mind, Nereus. She just doesn't know you yet, that's all."

I shrugged, feeling guilty. Ma thought I was upset, but in truth I was more relieved than disappointed that Hagne hadn't taken the bundle from me.

Charis shifted beside us. I looked round at her. In the excitement of Hagne's appearance I had almost forgotten the mage was with us. Charis was staring pensively after my sister, her mask dangling from her hand.

"Remarkable," the mage mused. "She has wild traits, certainly, yet she retains a solid sense of her own identity. She recognises people, she reads body language well, and she observes similarities between herself and others." Her fingers strayed to her own cheek. Then she turned to Ma. "And you were right. Her behaviour towards you is not dictated by mere self-interest. She shows real gratitude, real affection."

"She knows me," said Ma. "I could see it the first time she came out, and I still see it now. My Hagne isn't gone. Not entirely."

Charis rubbed her chin. "That speed… She has some ability to manipulate the miasma, I think. Yet she's not what is termed a mage. Her mind is too affected."

"She's no mage," Ma agreed, then hesitated. "Not yet."

Charis looked surprised, then thoughtful. "For someone to be affected so far and then to reemerge… I have never heard of it happening. But then, the cataphracts usually intervene before the chance arises." She gazed into the undergrowth again. "A slow change. A gradual assimilation." She nodded. "Yes, perhaps. Perhaps it is possible." She fixed Ma with a stern eye. "But do not let your hopes outstrip reality, Lya. It may be that Hagne will never improve further."

Ma squared her shoulders. "Well, if that is the case, it will change nothing. She is still my daughter."

A surge of pride ran through me. I'd never doubted that my mother was the best in the world, but now I saw she was even more amazing than I'd realised. Not only had she looked after me so well out here at the swamp's edge, but she'd been looking after my sister the whole time too.

I flung my arms around Ma's waist and hugged her tightly.

"Hello, Nereus." Ma embraced me in return. When we parted, I saw that Charis had turned away, head bowed. At first I thought she was wondering about Hagne again, but then a small, choked noise escaped her. She wasn't thinking. She was crying.

"You're upset," Ma exclaimed.

Charis wiped her eyes hurriedly. "My apologies. It is nothing."

"It is not nothing," Ma said.

Charis glanced at Ma. Then her eyes wandered to the swamp, and a sigh slipped from her. "It is just… Well. Hagne is lucky to have so dedicated a mother."

"Oh," Ma breathed. Releasing me, she stepped towards Charis, and this time I let her go.

Standing opposite the mage, Ma raised a hand to touch Charis's face. Charis twitched as if to turn away, but managed to stop the instinct. Ma's expression softened as her fingers met the mage's skin. She traced the line of Charis's cheek, the curve of her black-green lips. I watched, marvelling. At that moment, in the blue-green glow of the swamp, Ma's touch seemed to have some magic in it, her tenderness stripping away the horror of Charis's visage and revealing it as something else entirely. Not something ruined, but something precious. Not a thing to fear, but a thing to love.

Chapter Seven

From then on there were no more clandestine night walks. Ma visited Hagne in the daytime, in the morning right after we'd checked the traps for crawlers and moved any catches to the smoking shed. More often than not Charis and I went with her. Ma was always careful to dress me in the same protective outfit and let me wear the helm instead of the mage's homemade filter. Each time we went in, I felt a bit braver. I imagined myself as an explorer as I waded through poison-swollen plants and watched motes of pollen glitter beguilingly in the gloom. What would the village boys say if they could see me now? I almost wished I could tell them that I strayed regularly into the swamp, just to see the looks on their faces. I held my tongue, though. I knew how important it was that no one find out about my sister. The villagers would see her as a threat, an attacker and a thief lurking near their homes, and they'd send for a cataphract to hunt her down. No one would care that Hagne wasn't dangerous, that she looked at Ma with eyes full of love.

I held no illusions about cataphracts anymore. When I opened my book in the evenings, I disdained the tales of armoured killers and turned straight to the stories concerning mages. It was they who fascinated me now. Mages could influence the miasma, coaxing it out of those infected, extracting part of its essence to make filters. Not only that, but whatever it had done to them upon their first exposure meant that they could draw upon it to increase their agility and strength. And what about the contracts—how did those work? What else could mages do? The question no longer scared but intrigued me.

My sister grew braver with us too. She appeared more quickly when Ma called her, and her behaviour became less skittish. I still found her a little unsettling, and during our meetings I was always glad of Ma's presence at my side. Nevertheless, when the day came that Hagne finally took the bundle of supplies directly from my hands, I swelled with pride. I beamed up at Ma, forgetting that she wouldn't be able to see my grin beneath the helm. But she was also looking down at me, and despite the filter strapped over her face I knew that she was smiling too.

Charis and Hagne found each other fascinating. Charis spent long periods crouched beneath the blue-mottled tree, allowing Hagne to run her fingers over her face. Hagne murmured and frowned and pouted as she explored the mage's features, so similar to her own. Sometimes she would even giggle, and at those times I could clearly see in her joyful face the older sister who'd been lost to me. But no, not lost. Not yet.

A fortnight passed, and then another, and the mage remained with us. Eventually Ma broached the subject of her extended stay, though the way she asked made it clear she didn't want Charis to leave. Her relief at the mage's answer was obvious.

"The Council has not yet summoned me back," Charis said. "Until that happens, I shall do as I please."

As autumn passed, the worst of the heat broke and the rains began. Unlike the summer storms, which flung fat droplets to churn the ground, winter brought depressing drizzles that peppered your face and seemed to come from all directions at once. The sky lost its vivid tint and a pall descended, making our sagging house look merely old and wet rather than cosy and well-loved as it usually did. Only the swamp kept its colour. The changing weather did nothing to diminish the toxic plantlife. If anything, it cultivated more. New, strangely textured stalks wormed their way up from the mud to unfold into peculiar toothed flowers; thick vines spiralled higher up the tree trunks; pale squashy fungi popped up among the roots. The swamp, it seemed, thrived in every season.

Perhaps we should have seen this as a sign. Only the swamp would endure. Our tentative harmony could not withstand time in the same way.

Disaster struck one damp morning as we walked back to the house after visiting Hagne. I had run ahead of the adults, hungry for my breakfast, but as I neared the porch I spied two people approaching along the track. I halted in dismay. Though the figures were still some distance away, I recognised one of them instantly. Balx. There was no mistaking his broad outline, his stride that was almost a swagger. Yet beside Balx was an even more unwelcome sight. A figure mounted on a huge, amber-scaled reptile. A figure clad in dark, angular armour.

A cataphract.

For a moment I stood transfixed with shock. Then, pulling myself together, I dived into the long grass. Lying on my belly in the mud, I fumbled off the helm so as to make myself less noticeable. Head bare, I peered up again warily.

I couldn't help but be a little awed. The cataphract's reptile was bigger than Charis's mount, sturdier and with a longer neck and muzzle—a creature bred for hunting as well as travelling. Its clawed feet tore dirt from the track as it walked, its great wedge of a head swinging slowly from side to side with each stride. Even from this distance, I could see the yellow gleam of its eyes.

The cataphract sat straight and tall in the saddle, reins held loosely in one gauntleted hand. His armour encased him completely, but at the same time it emphasised the breadth of his shoulders, the span of his biceps. His helm was different to the one I held. Mine had a rounded crown, oval eyepieces, and a single central filter over the mouth area, which had been fashioned with a wire lattice and welded on. The cataphract's helm looked sleeker, somehow meaner. Two filters protruded to each side, and instead of wire they were formed by small holes punctured in the metal itself. The eyepieces were narrow and slanted, and the crown had been worked into a sharp crest so that it resembled the fighting ridge of his reptile. Over the cataphract's shoulder protruded the hilt of a broadsword.

My heart thundered against my ribs. We had only a few minutes before Balx and the cataphract arrived at the house. Behind me, I could just catch Ma and Charis's voices drifting through the rain.

I stumbled back to them in a semi-crouch, moving as fast as I could while staying low.

Fetching up before them, I gabbled my news.

"A cataphract! On the track! Balx and a cataphract—they're almost here!"

Ma's cheeks turned very pale, then very red. "Balx?" she repeated. "He wouldn't… He hasn't…" Her jaw clenched. "That bastard," she whispered. "And to think he pretended to care!"

Charis put a hand on her arm. "How far?" she asked me.

"They're at the bend!"

Ma fought down her fury with visible effort. Composure regained, she grasped my shoulders. "Go now, round the far side of the house, past the smoking shed. Do you have time to hide the helm?"

"I… I think so."

"Good. Do it. Then get indoors and take that gear off right away. We'll follow." She stripped her gloves and shoved them into a pocket, where she'd already stowed Charis's filter. "If they see us, we'll just say we've been out walking."

I nodded. My throat was too dry to speak.

"Go. Go now, Nereus."

I ran. Circling round the side of the house, I kept as much distance between myself and the approaching figures as possible. At the corner by the water butts, I peered cautiously round to check that I wasn't in sight of the track. The coast was clear. Thanking the Hale, I jogged along the planks to the water butts and hurriedly returned the helm to its place.

Inside the house, I yanked off my mud-caked boots and stuffed them under the bed, then shrugged off my jacket and gloves. Just in time—for as I stood on tiptoe to hang them back on their pegs, I heard voices outside.

Heart in mouth, I inched to the door and opened it.

Ma and Charis had almost managed to reach the house before Balx and the cataphract arrived, but had been halted at the base of the porch steps. Balx stood between them and the house. His back was turned to me, his meaty fists balled on his hips. Beside the trio, the cataphract loomed.

My clasp on the door handle slipped as my palms began to sweat. The cataphract was even more intimidating at close quarters. From afar I hadn't been able to see the dents and scratches that covered his armour, ingrained despite efforts to hammer and polish them out. The vestiges of countless fights, the evidence of victories. Sitting proud in his saddle, the cataphract wore them like decorations.

"…for a stroll," Ma was saying, then stalled as the cataphract kicked a leg over his reptile's back, landing with a squelch on the track. Mud splattered his greaves, but he gave it no mind. Releasing a clasp on his gorget, he removed his helm. The face revealed was alarmingly similar to the headpiece itself: a countenance of hard planes and straight lines, tempered to a tough finish. His hair was shaven at the sides in the warrior's style, his skin pallid and sun-deprived. His eyes were an arresting blue, though red-rimmed and rheumy. Despite the impressive look of his helm, it seemed the filters were less reliable than the one on the helm in our water butt.

"Lya Orbel?" he asked briskly.

Ma faced him calmly. "Lya Vestryn now, Sir. My husband gave up his name-right when he abandoned us. And you are?"

"My name is Sir Lysias of Pendarell." The cataphract made no bow, did not so much as offer a hand. "And you—" He addressed the mage. "—would be Charis Yondarin. Correct?"

The mage inclined her head, though only briefly.

Dithering on the threshold, I had so far remained unnoticed, but now the cataphract's reptile suddenly seemed to sense my presence. Its head snapped round and it snorted, nostrils expelling twin tendrils of breath into the drizzle.

All eyes turned to me. I shrank back in the doorway. "Hello," I croaked.

"This is Nereus," Ma said. "My son."

The cataphract granted me a cursory glance, appraising and dismissing me in the same instant, before returning his attention to Ma. "Mistress Vestryn, I have been called to investigate an accusation that has been brought against you." He gestured to Balx. "This man claims that you are harbouring a dangerous malignant."

"What?" I hadn't known Ma could playact so well; she sounded genuinely shocked. "But that's ridiculous. How would it even be possible? Malignants are wild. I couldn't hide one if I tried."

Lysias's gaze remained piercing. "He claims that you keep it in the swamp itself. That you visit it regularly with food and clothing." The cataphract paused. "That you have a helm."

I bit back a gasp. How did Balx know about the helm? Ma had never told him about it, I was certain. She hadn't even told me.

Ma blanched despite herself, and I could tell she was asking herself the same question. "That's absurd," she said, though her words did not have the same force as before. "Where would I come by such a thing?"

Lysias gave an elegant shrug. "It does seem to me unlikely, I confess." His reptile shifted; he placed a stilling hand on its flank. The gesture was somehow threatening. *I have power over this beast*, it seemed to say. *Do you think I don't have power over you?* "You are aware, of course, that the law forbids the use of a helm by anyone other than the cataphract for whom it was made?"

My tummy did a watery little flip. I'd known from Ma's secrecy that it was somehow naughty to have the helm, but I hadn't realised that every time we put it on we'd been breaking the law.

Ma stood her ground. "Of course."

Balx could no longer contain himself. He rounded on Ma. "I've seen it," he snapped. "I've seen you with it. I've seen the boy with it." He span to jab a finger at me. "They all go off into the swamp together."

Fury and fear rose within me. Had Balx been spying on us? I glared at him, but he had turned back to the cataphract.

Lysias's eyebrows rose. "If this is true," he told Ma, "the penalty will be severe."

Ma raised her chin. "It is not."

"She's lying!" Abruptly, Balx turned and thundered up the stairs. Before I had a chance to squirm away, he had hold of my arm and was dragging me across the porch, my feet slipping and slithering on the damp planks.

"Ow!" I squealed.

"Ask him," Balx demanded. "Ask the boy."

The cataphract's scrutiny fell upon me like a blade. "Is there any truth to this, boy? Does your mother have the helm of a cataphract? Do you visit a malignant in the swamp?" The reptile huffed and lowered its scaled head over its master's shoulder, regarding me along with him.

I was near frozen with terror, but I couldn't give in now. Ma was depending on me. Hagne was depending on me. I had to keep them safe.

"No," I said. My voice came out very small. I tried to make it bigger, surer. "No, Sir. I've never seen a helm, not 'til you came." An idea occurred to me, inspired by Ma's playacting. I pointed at the helm tucked under his arm. "Can I hold it, please, Sir?"

Balx hissed angrily through his teeth and his grip tightened on my arm. I winced, but inwardly I was smirking. If he would pull me about like a child then I would act like a child.

The cataphract snorted and, just as I hoped he would, turned away in dismissal. His attention settled upon Charis. "And you, Maestress. You also deny these accusations?" Upon his lips the honorific sounded like an insult.

Charis inclined her head. "There is no truth to them, Sir."

Balx thrust me away from him. His face had gone very red. "I've seen that helm, I swear," he cried. "If it isn't true, then why is she still here, eh?" He jabbed a finger at Charis. "It's been weeks since Lya fell ill. Why's the mage still sniffing around?"

"That," said Lysias, "is a pertinent question. Why are you still here, Yondarin? Your task is complete. Why haven't you reported back to the Council?"

"I do not swear fealty like you, Sir." Charis's reply had a chill edge. "My service to the Council does not bind me so strictly as it does your noble order." She half-grinned, half-grimaced. "In case you've forgotten, I am forbidden to take oaths in the name of the Hale."

The cataphract eyed her coldly. "I am well aware of the limitations of your kind," he said evenly. "Yet I wonder why you linger here. Why I find you out 'strolling' in the rain." His gaze dropped to Charis's mud-caked boots, then tracked slowly upwards. "Why I find you so shamelessly maskless."

Charis looked daunted for a moment. Then her lips tightened in anger. "The reason," she said, "is more obvious than you suppose." She reached out a hand to Ma, palm open, inviting. Ma took it without hesitation. Then Charis drew her close, and Ma folded herself into the contours of the mage's body.

In that instant, many things came clear to me—questions I hadn't even realised were questions found their answers. I thought of the tenderness with which the mage had nursed Ma back to health, the gentle way Ma had taken Charis's hand that time over breakfast, and that confused night when I had seen the mage's mask lying abandoned on the floor. I may only have been ten, but I recognised then what I'd been witnessing over the past weeks—the gradual burgeoning of a love affair, which even now was blossoming before my eyes.

I blinked, trying to work out how I felt. I waited for resentment, for anger, for all the feelings that had crowded in on me when Balx had been sniffing around Ma. They didn't come. Charis was not like Balx. Whereas he had treated Ma like a prize to be won and possessed, Charis looked at Ma with respect and tenderness. And Ma looked at her the same way.

The cataphract raised an eyebrow. Then his expression became stony. He turned to Balx, who was staring wide-eyed and appalled at the couple before him. "If I have travelled all this way to indulge the jealousy of a jilted lover, I will not take it kindly," Lysias told him. "To waste a cataphract's time on such a frivolous—"

"There is a helm!" Balx snarled. His face had twisted from shock into hate. "There is a helm here. I'll prove it!" Shoving me out of the way, he barged into the house. I sprawled against the railings.

"Hey!" Ma ran to my side. "What do you think you're doing?"

The only response was a clattering and crashing from inside the house. Charis hissed an oath, then leapt up the steps and raced through the door. Ma and I followed.

It had taken Balx only moments to devastate our front

room. The cupboards had been flung open and ransacked, the shelves rifled, the rug thrown out of place. Pots and pans lay strewn over the floor. Aghast, I saw my precious book lying among them, squashed open like a huge dead bug.

"My book!" I rushed to pick it up, cradling it carefully in my arms. The front board had come loose and some of the pages were crushed out of shape. Wrath bubbled within me. With a venomous glare at Balx, I returned the book to its rightful place on the plundered shelf, giving it a small pat of reassurance as I did so.

Balx noticed none of this. He'd wrenched open the door of the stove and was peering into its black interior.

"Get out of my house." Ma's words dropped like hailstones.

Balx withdrew his head. I took an involuntary step backwards, retreating against Ma's legs. Balx had always been cranky, but now he looked positively furious. As he climbed to his feet, the entirety of his substantial frame thrummed with ire. "Where is it?" he growled. "I know you've got it. Where are you hiding it, eh, Lya?"

Charis placed her rangy body between us and Balx. "Stop this," the mage said. "You will leave this inst—" Then her head snapped to one side as Balx backhanded her across the face.

"Out of my way, swamp-witch!"

Charis did not raise a hand to her cheek, did not so much as gasp at the impact of the blow. She merely paused for a moment, collecting herself. Then her feet shifted subtly and her fingers flexed. I recognised the fighting stance she'd used the first day she arrived. I gulped. Charis's powers against Balx's muscle—the struggle would be fearsome.

Thankfully, the cataphract chose that moment to duck through the door. His armour clanked as he stepped forward.

"Enough," he snapped. "Master Durran, this is no way to behave. You called me to conduct an investigation. Now permit me to do my job."

Faced with Lysias's authority, not to mention the sword at his back, Balx yielded grudgingly. He'd not given up though, and as his eyes shifted from Charis's face towards the cataphract, they suddenly fastened on something. Lunging past Lysias, he wrenched my jacket from its peg.

"There!" he cried. "It's damp!" He thrust the jacket under the cataphract's nose. "Feel that, Sir. The boy's been out recently too. They're holding back. They're lying to you." He came up short, a sudden greedy sheen colouring his features. "Damp…" he breathed.

Panic clutched me as Balx thundered back outside. Rushing out to the porch, I watched him descend the steps and begin rooting round the house, peering beneath the porch and kicking at the ground.

The others crowded out behind me. Ma folded her arms, trying to look scornful, though the lines around her eyes betrayed the tension beneath her act. "What do you hope to—" she began, only to be cut off as Balx gave a howl of triumph.

"Here!" he crowed. "It's here!" He reappeared from round the side of the house, holding the helm aloft.

The world went very still. To me, it seemed that even the insects stopped their droning, the rain crystallising as it fell. Then time restarted with a lurch as Lysias shouldered past us.

"Let me see it," he commanded.

Ma started forward with a strangled gasp, but Charis caught her hand. "No," the mage whispered. Was that resignation in her tone, or prudence? I hoped beyond hope that it was the latter, that she was forming some plan to get us out of this. I went to her, and Charis's other hand came down to rest lightly on my hair. There, together, we waited.

Lysias met Balx at the bottom of the steps. Taking the helm, the cataphract turned it over in his hands, much like Charis had done when I'd first shown it to her. After a few moments he froze. His breathing grew shallow, and he made another slower survey of the helm. Then his eyes narrowed, becoming steely slits. "Sir Gildas," he muttered. "By the Hale, *Sir Gildas*."

I frowned. Where had I heard that name? Then I remembered: Charis's story. Sir Gildas was the name of the cataphract who had hunted down those children, the cataphract who had left Charis for dead. And this… this was *his* helm? I wouldn't have believed it but for the way Charis's fingers had tensed against my scalp. The revelation made my stomach turn. I'd worn that helm, the same helm that had belonged to a cold-blooded child-killer. But how had it ended up here, hidden in our water butt? I looked up at Ma, searching for some clue in her face, but there was nothing there to help me. Her expression had closed like a toothcup snapped shut, the same way it closed when my father was mentioned.

"Sir Gildas," the cataphract repeated, his voice tinged with awe. "He was one of the citadel's most esteemed cataphracts… until he vanished ten years ago. A devastating loss. I was only a squire at the time, yet still I remember it. The confusion, the grief." Lysias's eyes misted with recollection. "Without the body, we couldn't even hold a proper funeral. There was a memorial of sorts, but what with the uncertainty…" He shook his head, his brow wrinkling. "They never did find out what had happened. He'd been called out to investigate a disturbance—some petty matter, I never did learn the details of it—and failed to return. It was somewhere in these parts, I recall." Lysias's gaze refocussed, sharpened. He raised his eyes to Ma. "I trust that you have an explanation for how you came to be in possession of his helm?"

Ma's reply was flat, defensive. "I know nothing of missing cataphracts. I found the helm at the edge of the swamp."

"Yet you did not report it."

Ma hesitated. This time no answer came.

"Why did you keep it?"

Ma remained silent.

Lysias ascended the steps, helm in hand. He came to within a foot of us, and there he stopped, an imposing figure encased in steel.

"I must conclude," the cataphract said softly, "that Master Durran has told me the truth. That you have been using this helm to make sorties into the swamp."

Ma shook her head, but still the denial would not emerge from her lips.

Lysias's hand fell to the scabbard of his broadsword. "Get back inside. All of you."

We did as we were told. The cataphract went to his reptile and drew a spool of cord from his saddlebags. Following us into the house, he arranged two chairs on opposite sides of the room and pointed Charis and Ma into them. Charis sank glumly onto one and, after a despairing glance at the mage, Ma seated herself on the other. I hovered wretchedly in the background as Lysias proceeded to bind them in place. Ma he tied to the chairback with her wrists bound behind; for Charis he used twice as much rope, even taking the extra precaution of securing her ankles to the chairlegs.

Then rough hands closed upon me, and I yelped in surprise as Balx lifted me clear of the floorboards.

Ma, who until now had sat despondent under Lysias's hands, started upwards. Her chair banged against the floor. "Leave him alone!" she cried. "He's a child, for Hale's sake."

"He's a troublemaker is what he is."

"Get away from him!"

Lysias raised a placatory hand, then examined me where I dangled in Balx's grip. It wasn't hard to look helpless beneath his scrutiny. After a moment, he nodded. "Leave the boy."

"But—"

"Leave him."

Balx released me reluctantly. I immediately scrambled over to Ma, falling by her side to hug her as best I could despite her bonds.

"Now, Master Durran," said Lysias, "I trust you to keep watch here until I return."

Balx frowned. "Where are you going?"

"My priority is the malignant." Lysias's hand moved to his sword again. He tapped one thumb upon the scabbard. "It must be dealt with at once."

"No!" Ma gasped. "No, please. Don't—"

Lysias cut her off. "You will gain nothing by pleading," he told her grimly. "No alternative can be considered. Malignants are a danger to our society. More than that, they are an affront to our Lord the Hale. By ancient decree, they cannot be allowed to roam free."

A sound bubbled from Ma's throat, half moan, half sob.

Lysias ignored her suffering. "When I return," he continued, "you will tell me everything about that helm. I will not accept silence, I will not accept evasions, and I certainly will not accept lies. If there is any further deception on your part, I will not be lenient."

The threat hung in the air as he departed, looming large in the ruins of our home. In the sudden hush, we heard the jingling of harness as the cataphract mounted his reptile and turned its head toward the swamp.

As the sound died away, Ma's spirit seemed to go out of her. Her chin sagged to her chest.

I tightened my embrace, pressing my face into her side. "Ma," I whispered. "Ma."

But there was no comfort I could offer her now.

Chapter Eight

"I didn't want this for you, Lya."

It was Balx who broke the silence. He'd dragged a chair against the front door and sat upon it facing us. Just looking at him made my head throb with anger. Grampa had made that chair. Balx had no right to sit on it and certainly no right to hold us captive in our own home. I wanted to scream at him, knock him to the ground, throw him out over the porch and see him go face-first in the mud with the crawlers. I wished I was bigger, older, stronger. But I wasn't. I could do nothing except cling to Ma and glare at our enemy out of the corner of my eye.

Ma did not answer him, though I felt her stiffen.

Balx drummed one ankle on the floorboards, knee jiggling up and down. "This isn't what I wanted," he repeated. "It isn't how I imagined things turning out."

"Oh?" Ma raised her face to him. Her eyes were red-rimmed behind a curtain of hair. "And what did you imagine?"

Balx passed a hand across his brow. "I thought we had an understanding," he said. A bewildered resentment coloured his words. "All that time. Me coming here to help you out. Bringing wood, bringing milk…"

Ma shook her head. "I never asked you to do that. I never asked for anything."

Balx's jaw clenched. He ploughed on, ticking off points on his fingers. "Fixing the shed roof," he insisted, "mending the guttering, taking you to the market with your baskets…" He threw up his hands. "I thought we were friends, Lya."

"So did I." Ma's reply was low with its own bitterness. "It seems we were both mistaken."

A flush darkened Balx's cheeks. "It seems so. It seems so." He sat grinding his teeth for a few seconds. Then his resentment boiled over. He beat a fist on his thigh, voice rising. "What happened, Lya, eh? All I did was help you. I was good to you, Lya. But as soon as this freak arrives I'm ordered away—out of favour, just like that. As if I was nothing to you. As if I was nothing at all."

Ma weathered the tirade with weary calm. "I don't owe you anything, Balx."

"Don't owe— Fah! I know what I'm owed, Lya, and that's some damn respect!" Balx's outburst propelled him to his feet. He lurched across to the table where Lysias had placed the ill-fortuned helm. "And this! Then this comes to light." He swivelled to face us again, finger prodding at the air as though squashing invisible flies. "I see you with this, and I realise Mistress Vestryn isn't as virtuous as she makes out. A helm, of all things! Where did you get it, eh?"

When Ma did not answer, Balx's cheeks deepened to crimson. He swayed on his feet, drunk on indignation. "She's corrupted you," he decided. "This swamp-witch has corrupted you. That's it, isn't it? She's done something to you. Ensorcelled you."

"No," said Ma.

"Why else would you choose her?" Balx looked at Charis, mouth twisting. She returned his gaze balefully. "Why else would you choose *that*?"

I felt Ma's breathing quicken in anger, but her voice remained measured as she replied, "You wouldn't understand, even if you wanted to. You don't have the capacity."

Balx looked murderous. "It's obscene," he spat. "It's revolting. More than that, it's absurd. You barely know each other."

"Charis knows me better than you ever could."

"Ungrateful whore!"

The blow took Ma off-guard. I screamed as the force of it teetered her chair, tearing my arms from around her waist. A moment later, the chair rocked back into place. Ma let out a whimper of pain.

Balx leaned over her, chest heaving. I cringed away as he hissed in her ear. "I could have you right now. Right here."

Charis's voice rang out cold and clear across the room. "Touch her again and I will pull your entrails out through your nose and string them up with the snakes in the smoking shed."

For the briefest moment Balx looked unnerved. Then he seemed to remember that the mage was his prisoner, and the confidence returned to his face. He rounded on her, though I noticed that he dared not venture close. "I could do the same to you," he snarled, "did not the thought make me want to puke."

"You're a brute." Ma looked up at Balx. Her hair fell away from her face, exposing the bruise that was already spreading, rot-hued, across her cheek. "And you're surprised that I don't want you?"

Her bitterness was such that you could almost taste it. Even

Balx was taken aback. The sight of her face seemed to unman him; he glanced at his hands as though scared of what they'd done. He backed away to hover again by the table, where he cast about, searching for a way to regain control. The helm offered him one.

"When Lysias returns, he'll teach you," he growled. "You'll be in for it then. And whatever… creature you have hidden away in that swamp will be dead and gone."

Ma sucked in a breath, and I felt her start to tremble as she fought back tears.

I couldn't stand it any longer; my entire body was quivering with rage and hatred. Springing to my feet, I launched myself at Balx. It no longer mattered that I was small and he was big. I wanted only for his cruelty to stop. "Leave us alone!" I cried. "Why can't you leave us alone!"

Balx swept me up like a bug in a net. In instants my back had hit the wall and I found myself pinned there with a great hand squeezing my throat. My legs dangled uselessly, heels scraping the wood.

Ma let out a shout of protest. Balx ignored her. His lip curled as I squirmed in his grip. "Another word out of you," he said, "and I'll throw you into the swamp myself." He released me abruptly and I thumped to the floor, gasping.

When Ma spoke, her voice had gone timorous. "Nereus," she murmured, "why don't you go read your book?"

I staggered to my feet. No. I wouldn't leave her, not bound like this, not with Balx. "No," I croaked. "I don't want—"

"I think you should," Ma interjected.

I gazed at her in dismay. *Don't send me away. Not this time.* I tried to plead with her through my eyes alone. *I want to stay with you, Ma.*

But her face was firm, as it was when I had a chore to do and no protests would prevent it. And suddenly I realised that she was also trying to tell *me* something. She saw me realise, and her eyebrow twitched in encouragement.

She turned to Balx. "Can he?" she asked him, quiescent now. "Go read his book in the bedroom?"

Balx grunted. Ma's new meekness seemed to appease him. "If it'll stop him squealing." He cuffed me on the back of the head, sending me stumbling back across the room. "Go on, get out of my sight. Idiot boy."

I still didn't understand. What good would my book do? "But—"

"Fetch your book, Nereus." Ma's command was almost a plea. At a loss, I glanced at Charis. As ever, the mage's face was hard to read, but I thought I saw a flicker of acknowledgement in her dark eyes, a flicker that said: *Do it*.

Ma's chair had been pushed up against the shelf on which the books were kept. Shoulders drooping, I edged round the chair and knelt to take the volume from its place. As I did so, something brushed my arm and, looking down, I saw that Ma was holding something scrunched in her hands.

The filter.

It was all I could do not to gape. Ma must have been easing it out of her pocket this whole time; my struggle with Balx must have provided enough distraction for her to free it completely. Now she was holding it out to me, her bound hands pressing against my arm.

Understanding came in a rush, and with it resolve. I took the filter from Ma, slipping it quickly beneath the storybook so that when I held the volume to my chest the filter was cushioned between the book and my body.

"Hurry up, boy," Balx warned.

I plodded to the bedroom with my head down, pretending reluctance. At the door I glanced back. Both Ma and Charis's eyes were upon me, and now I could read their message clearly.

Go, Nereus. Go now. Warn your sister before it's too late.

In the bedroom, I pulled the door half-closed and put the book down on the mattress. Then, as quietly as I could, I retrieved my dirty boots that, earlier, I'd hidden beneath the bed. I pulled them on swiftly and, avoiding the creakiest of the floorboards, tiptoed to the window. Thank the Hale for Balx's temper—in his pique he'd forgotten there was another way out of this room. I had to be quick though. Balx was a hothead, not a fool. At any moment he might realise his mistake.

Thankfully the shutters were already open, though the drizzle had peppered the sill and I had to take care not to slip as I climbed onto the ledge and jumped out. I landed with a splat, rain and mud stippling my shirt. I paused for a moment, listening, but could hear nothing. There came no cry of outrage, no thundering footsteps. I swallowed. The quiet was spooky. What was Balx doing in there? I was tempted to rush back in, to check what was happening to Ma and Charis. But then I spotted the reptile tracks.

The combined weight of the cataphract and his mount had carved deep prints in the sludgy ground, the three-clawed furrows forming an ominous path away from the house.

Hagne. My sister needed me more than Ma did.

There was no time to be scared. I set off towards the swamp, tying Charis's filter round my face as I went.

Chapter Nine

Lysias's tracks disappeared as they approached the swamp, swallowed by the mud that grew only deeper as it neared the line of trees. Beyond that, there was no sign of the cataphract. His reptile had taken him far ahead.

The thought prompted a jolt of panic. Lysias was already in the swamp, already crashing through the trees with his sword in hand, hunting for my sister. I forced my legs to move faster, plunging my feet into the sucking mud and yanking them out again. My thighs began to ache almost immediately, but I gritted my teeth and pushed on. This was no time to feel sorry for myself. I had to hurry. I had to warn Hagne to get away before Lysias found her first.

At least the route to the blue-mottled tree wasn't obvious to a stranger's eye. Ma had always been careful to vary the places we entered the swamp, so there were no obvious signs to point the way to my sister's usual haunt. Luckily, I'd been to the clearing enough times to find my way. Heading to the nearest familiar entry point, I plunged in. The light dimmed, the heat closed around me, and the heady odour of the swamp reached my nostrils through the filter.

It was only after a minute or so of pushing through the

foliage that I realised I hadn't hesitated before entering the swamp. My own intrepidness took me aback. Despite my many visits here I'd never been into the swamp without Ma, not since that first disastrous time when I'd taken the helm. I'd never contemplated entering alone since. Today it seemed that my fear for my sister had overwhelmed my fear of the miasma.

You will have to be brave. That's what Charis had told me, on that morning when so many truths had come to light. Was this bravery, then? This sweating, panting, heart-in-mouth desperation? Was this how Ma had felt on that long-ago day when Hagne first vanished into the swamp? And was this how she had felt later, when she thought that I had done the same?

I'd never thought I was like Ma. The prospect swelled my courage. I could do this. I could do this for Hagne and for Ma, and for Charis too. I could do this for my family, just like Ma had done before me, and would be doing right now if not for Balx.

I soldiered on, taking the route I knew would come out at Hagne's tree. I moved as fast as I could through the treacherous vegetation, though even in my urgency I knew I had to be careful. I was only in my shirt and trousers; I didn't even have my jacket or gloves to shield me from grazes and cuts. So as I ventured deeper and the foliage became thicker, I was forced to slow, ducking under low branches and stepping gingerly round thorny stems. At one point my boot almost disappeared into a patch of bog, and I had to fight to keep myself calm as I drew it slowly out, remembering what Charis had once told me about struggling making you sink faster.

The decrease in speed was agonising. I couldn't stop picturing Lysias hacking and slashing his way through the swamp, swift and deadly on his reptile's back. But I didn't have

armour, or a helm, or a sword. The only things that stood
between me and the miasma were Charis's handmade filter
and a few flimsy layers of clothing. I had no choice but to
wend my way with care. It would do Hagne no good if I was
cut and poisoned.

Finally, when my heart was about ready to burst with
anxiety, I stumbled into the clearing and saw the tree. I stood
for a moment beneath it, wondering what to do. Ma's pan still
hung from the branch. Dare I strike it, summon my sister that
way? The sound-deadening quality of the swamp might work
in my favour; I'd heard nothing of Lysias yet, after all. I took
up a stick, raised it to hit the pan, then hesitated. How stealthy
could a cataphract be, moving through swampland? Lysias had
been trained for this his whole life; perhaps I wouldn't hear
him coming. And how good was a reptile's hearing?

I lowered the stick. I couldn't risk it.

Instead, I tiptoed to the edge of the clearing and hissed
Hagne's name, then stood scouring the bushes for movement.
She did not come. I tried again, calling as loudly as I dared.
There was still no sign of her. I fought down my fear, telling
myself that she often took a while to appear. Still, doubts
crowded my mind. Had she even heard me? She must make
her home somewhere near the tree, but surely she didn't stay
here all the time. What if she'd wandered off? What if Lysias
had already found her?

I hissed Hagne's name a few more times, hopping from
foot to foot as I waited. Nothing. Tears blurred in my eyes.
With every minute that passed, I became more convinced that
it would not be Hagne who appeared but Lysias, wielding a
sword stained with my sister's blood.

A soft noise behind me made me yelp. I clapped my hands

over my mouth and pivoted, then heaved a sigh of relief to see Hagne standing behind me—she must have jumped down from the tree again. She grinned at me with yellowing teeth, amused by my shock. Then she saw my empty hands and her brow wrinkled. She looked round the clearing, and her confusion increased when she saw I was alone.

"Hagne," I gasped. "You have to get away from here. There's a man—he's hunting you. He can't be far away."

She tilted her head at me, brow wrinkling further.

I gestured into the trees, away from the house, away from Lysias's stalking ground. "You have to leave this place," I told her. "Go away, far away! There's a man coming, a bad man. He'll kill you if he finds you!" I tried to get across the urgency without raising my voice too much; who knew what damage my startled yelp might already have done. But Hagne only regarded me in consternation. I couldn't tell if she'd understood anything at all.

"We don't have much time," I said. Stepping forward, I chanced taking her hand. She started at the contact, then gazed at me with even greater perplexity. I tugged at her. "You have to go," I insisted. I pointed into the depths of the swamp, flinging out my arm for emphasis. "Go far away from here, to a different part of the swamp. Stay away for a while. Hide until it's safe again."

She strayed with me a few steps and then stopped, craning her neck round again to peer in the direction I'd come.

I squeezed her hand. "Ma's not coming," I told her. "Ma can't come. It's only me, Hagne. You have to listen to me."

My sister's lips parted and a distressed sound slipped out, plaintive and bewildered. It was a sound I'd made myself when I woke at night in darkness and fear and wanted nothing else than for Ma to comfort me. In my case, Ma had always been at my side, ready to soothe me with soft kisses and tender hands. But here, now, Hagne and I were on our own. Ma could not pluck us from danger, not this time.

Even as the thought crossed my mind, I heard something away to our right: crunching and swishing, as of greenery being crushed underfoot.

"No!" I gasped. "Hagne, come on!" I yanked at her, but she only dug her bare heels into the mud. She was surprisingly strong for someone so skinny. She cocked her head in the direction of the sound, curious and expectant.

"That's not Ma!" My voice wobbled, close to a sob. "We have to go, Hagne! We have to hide! We have to—"

But it was too late. My words were cut off as Lysias and his reptile appeared through the trees, erupting into the clearing in a torrent of metal and scales. The cataphract spotted us immediately. Pulling on the reins, he brought his reptile to an abrupt halt. It snorted, yellow eyes narrowing to twin slits. Upon its back, the slatted eyepieces of Lysias's helm mirrored his reptile's gaze. He reached over his shoulder and drew his sword.

I stood frozen, still clasping my sister's hand, too horrified even to back away. There was no escaping this. Towering above us in his armour and helm, the cataphract looked inhuman—a being of pure metal and unalloyed, impenetrable purpose. Begging would do us no good. There were no cracks in his armour through which mercy might penetrate.

With a press of his heels, Lysias urged the reptile forward. But in the same instant, my sister sprang into action. Disentangling her hand from mine, she turned and shoved me towards the tree. I let out a startled cry as I staggered away from her, then managed to catch myself on the trunk. Blue moss flaked away on my hands. Regaining my balance, I whipped round to find out what was happening.

What I saw made me gape. Hagne had sprung to my defence: one scrawny swamp-girl against a cataphract and his hulking reptile. As I watched, she easily dodged Lysias's first swipe and then ducked beneath his second, rolling to the side and coming to her feet in one smooth movement. Then she leapt nimbly away again as the reptile's head darted in for a bite, leaving its jaws to snap on empty air.

"Hagne," I breathed, half in horror, half in wonderment. Her speed was mesmerising. It was also the only thing keeping her alive. For as the cataphract recovered from his initial surprise, he became the machine he so resembled. The broadsword moved dark and swift through the half-light, inscribing deadly, efficient arcs. Hagne was hard-pressed to avoid the blade, not to mention the teeth and claws and crest of the reptile. Trained along with its rider, the beast too fought with brutal purpose.

If it hadn't been so deadly, it might have seemed like a dance: the sword gleaming in Lysias's hand, the reptile's scales shimmering as it lunged and snapped, Hagne's bare limbs flickering in and out of sight as she leapt through the dappled shade. I tried to keep my eyes on my sister but her agility made it almost impossible. Yet, in the glimpses I caught of her, I thought I noticed something—something moving beneath her skin. Something faintly pulsing. Something faintly silver. Something that looked a little like caterpillars.

My breath caught. My sister was calling on the miasma's power just like Charis had done. A spark of hope alighted within me. If Hagne could control the miasma, maybe she had a chance. Maybe, like the mage, she could make herself stronger. Maybe she could win.

But Hagne did not have Charis's gifts, not yet. In dismay I saw the silver veins fade before they could manifest, and then Hagne screamed as the cataphract's blade found its target, slashing across her ribs. She stumbled, narrowly avoiding a bite from the reptile, then fell on her back. The reptile loomed over her, teeth bared, but Lysias yanked its head back and spoke a word of command. The reptile stilled immediately.

In the sudden quiet, Lysias dismounted and strode towards Hagne, blade poised in one gauntleted hand.

"No!" Before I knew what I was doing, I had raced out to plant myself between the cataphract and my sister. My heart was pounding like a drum and I felt like I was going to wet myself, but I couldn't let this happen. Hagne had fought for me, trying to keep me out of danger. I couldn't leave her to her fate.

"Leave her alone," I said.

"Nereus." The voice that reverberated from beneath the helm was full of dreadful echoes. "Step away from the malignant."

Sweat dripped down my face, soaking into the makeshift filter, but I did not move away. Perhaps if I stayed here he wouldn't attack. Cataphracts were supposed to be protectors, after all. They were lawkeepers, guardians, bound by an oath to the Council and the Hale. Then I remembered Charis's story. Never mind mages' arcane abilities, I did not know what cataphracts were capable of.

Still, I did not move. I listened to my sister's breathing behind me—shallow and panicky with exhaustion and pain—and I remained standing between her and her would-be murderer.

Lysias's fingers shifted on the hilt of his sword. "Sheltering a malignant is a crime, Nereus. You know this."

"I won't let you hurt her."

"She is an animal. A dangerous animal."

"No." I shook my head. "No." Lysias's reptile was a dangerous animal. Hagne was not like that. Hagne was… "She's my sister," I whispered. Even as I said it, I felt certainty well in my chest. The truth of the words bolstered my courage. Like the contract I'd struck with the mage, they seemed binding in a manner beyond speech. They could not be betrayed. "She's my sister."

Lysias's tone darkened. "You will be punished for your involvement here, boy. Do not think your age will hold back the Council's justice."

He was trying to scare me away. Moments before, it might have worked. Not now. Now I was set on my course. Hagne was family, and you did not abandon family, no matter what.

Behind Lysias, his reptile let out a hiss. Hagne hissed weakly back.

Lysias's arm twitched impatiently. "Enough of this," he grunted. Before I even saw it coming, he had swiped out with the flat of his blade, batting me aside. The next thing I knew I was lying with my face in the mud, bruised and winded and wheezing.

"No…" I spluttered. I struggled to my feet, but it was only to see the point of the cataphract's sword now a mere inch from Hagne's throat. She lay staring up at him, anger and fear swimming in her eyes. Pinned.

Lysias's next words were cutting as his blade. "Do not interfere again, boy. Or this time, you will get hurt."

The cataphract drew back his arm, ready for the strike. But

before he could bring his blade down, more crashing sounded through the foliage.

Lysias spun on his heel. "What—"

Another reptile burst into the clearing. It was smaller and rangier than Lysias's mount, with grey-green scales, and on its back it carried two riders. Its pace did not slow as it charged across the clearing and barrelled into Lysias, throwing the cataphract aside. Lysias's mount screeched and started forward, but the other reptile whipped round and roared, its neck-frill unfurling to reveal a mane of fearsome scarlet webbing. Intimidated, Lysias's reptile danced backwards.

My heart almost burst with relief. "Ma! Charis!"

It was like a rescue from a story. Charis's uncovered face was grim and determined as she gripped her reptile's reins. Ma was mounted behind her. She wore the helm, and though she was armed only with a kitchen skillet she looked every bit the avenging warrior.

As Lysias struggled, cursing, back to his feet, Ma and Charis slid off the reptile's back. The mage ran swiftly to the cataphract's mount. The huge beast snapped at her, but she evaded its jaws with a practised swerve and ducked in close to its head. Her fingers worked over its flank, and she leaned close to mutter in its ear. The reptile shifted, huffed a little, and then calmed.

Meanwhile, Ma approached Lysias. The cataphract had somehow managed to keep hold of his sword, and as he moved forward to confront Ma he held the blade low and steady. Ma did not quail. Clasping her skillet in front of her like a weapon, she squared up to the cataphract in the half-light. An instant later Charis joined her, standing at her shoulder in a fighting stance. Silver tendrils were already creeping over her hands, webbing the palms with power.

Hagne lay between them, hissing quietly in pain. Black blood stained her shift where Lysias had slashed her.

"You dare…" Lysias was almost incoherent in his fury. "You dare attack a cataphract of the citadel?"

"Get away," said Ma, "from my daughter."

"You are mad!" Lysias exclaimed. "She is no daughter of yours anymore."

"You have no idea what you are talking about."

"She cannot live," Lysias said. "Malignants must be exterminated. The law of this land—the law of the Hale— decrees it."

Ma shook her head. "The law decrees that malignants who are a danger to society cannot live. Not that none of them can."

"You are deluded, woman." Lysias stepped forward, the point of his sword rising slightly. Hagne twisted her head at his footfall. Seeing him approach, she levered herself up on her elbow. She stayed like that for a few seconds, but it was too much for her. She collapsed back upon the soil and lay there wincing and snarling in frustration.

Lysias snorted. "You see? She is wild. She is dirty. She is also wounded. So let us be done with this charade. It will be kinder to end her now."

"Stop right there," Ma warned. "Move another step and you will find out what happened to the last cataphract who threatened my child."

It took a moment for her words to sink in. Then Lysias's blade wavered as surprise shook him. "What are you saying? That you…" He faced her, helm to helm. "No," he breathed. "You… Sir Gildas…?"

"It was my husband who summoned him." Ma's voice

sharpened with anger and grief. "Summoned a cataphract to slay his own daughter, then fled before Sir Gildas even arrived. A coward, giving up on his own child and then running away from the consequences." She paused. "I couldn't allow it."

Lysias's reply was scornful. "You expect me to believe that you, alone, dispensed with Sir Gildas, victor of countless battles, ten-time winner of the Golden Lance?" He scoffed. "No. You are lying."

"There are more ways to defeat an enemy than with a sword."

"With a skillet, perhaps?"

Ma raised her chin. "Think what you like, Sir, but this helm did not come to me by chance."

Doubt crept in on Lysias; his weight shifted, and even in his armour he seemed to shrink a little.

As for me, I was flabbergasted. So that was the real secret of the helm. Ma hadn't just found it—she had taken on a cataphract in defence of her daughter. And she had won.

Courage surged through me. I looked at Lysias and saw that I'd been wrong about him before. He was not impenetrable. He was not mighty. He was just a man in fancy armour.

And right now, he was distracted. Ma's words had lowered his guard. He had forgotten all about the mud-covered boy behind him.

I acted before I could lose heart. With a cry, I launched myself upon the cataphract's back and wrapped my arms around his helm. He roared in surprise and swung his sword up, but I was too close for him to strike me and the blade merely whooshed past my shoulder. He pivoted blindly, trying instead to shake me off. I braced myself, but as he span round my hands slipped apart and I lost my grip on his helm.

I grabbed instead at his neck, scrabbling for purchase, and succeeded in catching hold of his gorget. Dimly, I heard Ma shout my name.

Then something clicked and loosened beneath my fingers. There was a wrench, a hiss of air escaping, and suddenly I was falling. I toppled back, landing again in the mud. Something landed on top of me. I looked to see what it was, then gasped.

His helm.

"Give it back!" In instants Lysias was upon me. He'd flung his sword aside; all his efforts were concentrated on retrieving the helm I now held. He would have got it too, had not Charis chosen that moment to join the fray, pulling Lysias off me and tackling him to the ground. The cataphract tried to resist her, but in doing so his leg bent wrongly beneath him. There came a wince-inducing crack, and Lysias let out an agonised yelp. Seizing her moment, Charis got astride him and pinned him into the mud.

"Hagne!" The skillet dropped with a dull thud as Ma rushed to my sister's side, falling to her knees beside her. Her hands hovered over Hagne's bloodstained shift. Then, ripping a strip from the hem of her skirts, she began to bind the wound. "It's going to be all right," she murmured. "I'm here now, Hagne. I'm here." My sister squirmed and grimaced, but allowed Ma to continue.

Meanwhile, I retreated from the struggling cataphract, scooting away on my bottom with the helm still cradled in my lap. I couldn't quite believe what I'd just done.

"My helm!" Lysias was shouting. "I command you to return my helm!" Lying there in the mud, he was almost unrecognisable from the composed warrior who had arrived at our porch earlier that morning. Sweat plastered his hair to his scalp, and his features were twisted in fury. He bucked against Charis's grip, but despite his warrior's strength he could not dislodge the mage's hold. Here, in the very heart of the miasma's realm, her power pulsed much brighter than it had in the confines of our house. The silver veins cast a ghostly glow around the scene.

When Lysias realised he was trapped, his wrath intensified. "You think you will go unpunished?" he spat, aiming the words like projectiles at Charis and Ma. "For defying a cataphract? And for murdering another? You think you will not feel the bite of a blade for this?"

Calmly, Ma finished binding Hagne's wound. "One day I will pay for what I've done," she said. "But it is a price I will pay gladly, for I will be paying it for my children." She tied off Hagne's bandage with a firm tug. Then her gaze moved to Lysias. "But you also have a price to pay, Sir Lysias of Pendarell." Her voice had become cold and terrible. She stood and walked to where Lysias's broadsword lay discarded on the ground. The weapon would have been too heavy for a village woman to lift, but years of solitary toiling had made my mother strong. She picked up the sword and levelled it at Lysias. "Move away, Charis. This man must pay for his actions."

Ma advanced on the cataphract, but Charis did not move. "Wait," the mage said. She looked up at Ma, black eyes inscrutable. "There is a better way."

For a moment anger clouded Ma's face. Then trust wiped the emotion away and she nodded, dropping the swordpoint to the earth.

Charis turned to address the cataphract. "Everything has a price, Sir. You have dealt death to many who have not deserved it, and death would be one price to pay for such actions. But there is another way. A way that will help you to truly understand what you have done." Then the mage looked to me. "Nereus, give the helm to your mother."

Colour drained from Lysias's face as realisation dawned. "No… You mustn't… You can't…" His eyes sought me out where I sat in the mud. "Nereus, no. You must give it to me. To me." His voice firmed as he spoke. "Listen to me, boy. This has gone quite far enough. I am a cataphract of the citadel, acting in the service of the Council. You must give the helm to me."

I found myself shaking. Despite what he'd been about to do to my sister, it was hard to disobey Lysias. Though he lay helpless in the mage's grip, the Council's authority echoed beneath his words.

But what was the Council to me? I'd never been to the citadel where they sat in state, and I was not likely to go. I had a vague idea of a magnificent council chamber enshrined in the centre of a great walled city—an image gleaned from my storybook—but that was all. The Council seemed a thousand leagues away from me here, where I sat in the miasmic twilight of the swamp. They might as well have *been* a story for all the good they had done us.

No. Charis was right: everything had a price. And it was not always the laws of the Council that decided what that price should be.

I picked myself out of the mud. Then, taking a deep breath, I walked past the cataphract to hand the helm to Ma. She took it wordlessly, acknowledging my decision with a hand placed, briefly, upon my head.

I went then to Hagne. Ma had tucked some torn-off rags beneath her head so that it was propped up slightly from the ground. My sister looked much happier now that her injury was bound. She smiled at me as I squatted beside her, and when I took her hand she stroked a finger down my wrist.

Lysias's composure finally fell apart. "Give it back!" he screamed. "For the Hale's sake, give it back!"

Charis remained stern. "I do not think so," she said. Then, in one fluid movement, the mage let go of Lysias, unfolding to her feet and backing away. Lysias tried to grab her legs but she had already stepped out of reach.

"Give me—" The cataphract attempted to stand, but as he put weight on his broken leg it crumpled again. He screeched and fell back in a clank of armour.

Ma and Charis came over to us and together we moved to the reptiles. Ma led me to Lysias's erstwhile steed and helped me onto its back. The beast did not complain; whatever Charis had whispered to it, it was now perfectly docile. It was Hagne's turn next, Ma and Charis lifting her carefully onto the mage's reptile. Charis mounted up behind my sister, putting her arms around Hagne to steady her, while Ma did the same with me.

Lysias watched our preparations with wide, wild eyes. "Wait…" he moaned. "Please, you can't leave me here. The miasma… I'll die."

"You might die," Charis informed him. "But then again, you might not." She tweaked her reptile's reins, turning its head away. "It is more of a chance than you gave those before you. It is more of a chance than you were willing to give Hagne."

"Better to kill me!" Lysias howled. "Better dead than malignant."

"Then you must hope for the best." Charis indicated her own face and smiled grimly. "And you must hope that others have mercy where you did not."

Then she dug her heels into her reptile's flanks, nudging it into a sloping trot. Ma and I did the same, following her out of the clearing.

As Lysias's cries faded behind us, Ma brought our reptile alongside Charis's. "If he lives, he could be a danger to us," she said softly.

Charis glanced over. "That's as may be. There is always a contract. Always a price."

I realised I was crying. I wiped the tears away on my sleeve, but it did no good. They kept falling, though I could not work out what I was crying for. Relief for Hagne? Fear for myself? Pity for Lysias?

"Ma," I whispered shakily. "What will we do? Are we going back to the house?"

I felt Ma shake her head. "It's time for us to go," she said. "We would have to leave the house sooner or later. And besides, I doubt that Balx has left much for us to salvage. He won't be in a good mood when he comes to. Charis gave him quite a knock when she got us free."

"But… But…" There was so much to say, so much to ask. How would we survive? Where would we go? Would anyone help us? But the only question that came to my lips was a stupid one. "Can't I get my book?"

Ma leaned close to my ear. "You're past those stories, Nereus. It's time to find some new ones, don't you think?"

Then Ma slipped the reins into my hands, though she kept her fingers curled lightly round my own.

Discover Luna Novella in our store:

Printed in the USA
CPSIA information can be obtained
at www.ICGtesting.com
JSHW020828200124
55354JS00005B/184